THE
FIERY
ISLAND

SHEILA SPENCER-SMITH

Scripture Union
130 City Road London EC1V 2NJ

By the same author
Past Tense – Impressions series

© Sheila Spencer-Smith 1994
First published 1994

ISBN 0 86201 833 1

British Library Cataloguing-in-Publication Data.
A catalogue record for this book is available from the British Library.

Phototypeset by Intype, London
Printed and bound in Great Britain by Cox & Wyman Ltd, Reading.

For Matthew, Jonathan, Geoffrey, Michael and Julian

Chapter One

The sea sparkled silver as the boat splashed through the waves near the beach.

'The island!' Toby shouted. 'Our own Treasure Island. Uncle Alec, are you *sure* we'll have it all to ourselves?'

His uncle looked solemn, but he winked at Lynette as he steered the boat through the shimmering sea. 'Guaranteed, laddie. No one ever comes here but me, and I'm only here today to maroon you two.'

'And if you don't come back for us we'll have to stay here for ever?'

'For sure. And maybe you'll have to deal with a band of pirates, too, all on your own.'

'Oh *Uncle Alec!*' Lynette said severely, but she couldn't help laughing. 'Don't encourage him.'

The boat nosed forward onto the sand, and Toby was out at once with his sailing book clutched in one hand. He took the rucksack from Lynette as she jumped out too.

'Have fun!' Uncle Alec called as he pushed off with one oar.

They watched until the boat was a small dot in the distance. Then Toby let out a resounding yell, and did three handstands in quick succession before racing across the beach to the rocks and cliff on the other side.

Lynette couldn't hear what he was shouting, but it didn't matter. Nothing mattered in this brilliant place.

She took a deep satisfied breath. It seemed light years away from the new city parish in England that Mum and Dad were visiting at this very moment, and the worrying changes that would come when Dad became vicar of St George's Church there. The only things on the island were rocks and sand and heather... and themselves. Incredible as it seemed ... only themselves!

Toby came rushing back. 'I've found a good place by the cliffs. We could build a hide-out.'

'I'm going to explore first.' Lynette looked up at the bare hill behind them. 'Come on.'

It was hard work pushing up through the heather with the sun hot on her face, but with her longer legs she got to the top first.

'Look, Toby,' she gasped. 'Look at the Mellon Isles out there. They're like jewels on the blue sea. I've never seen anything like it.'

Toby gazed at them too, his eyes full of longing. 'I wish we had a boat of our own so we could sail out to them.'

He clutched his sailing book, and Lynette knew that he would study it even harder now in case a miracle happened and they got a boat. The wind ruffled his brown hair and he raised his head. 'It's getting stronger,' he cried. 'I bet the weather's rough here sometimes. I'd like to be here in a gale.'

Lynette laughed as she threw herself down on the heather. As far as she could see on the other side of the water there was nothing except rocky coastline and the lonely cottage that belonged to their uncle and aunt above the tiny deserted harbour.

'We're the only people for miles and miles,' she said in satisfaction. 'Coronsay. That's a good name for this island. We can come here every day for as long as we're here, and ...'

Suddenly Toby let out a yell that had her leaping up, her heart pounding. 'Over there ... look!'

A red-sailed dinghy was coming out of the small harbour on the mainland.

Lynette sank to the ground again, and sat with her arms round her knees. 'Oh Toby, is that all? I thought it was something terrible, the island on fire at least.'

Her brother's cheeks were flushed with excitement. 'There's a girl at the helm, and she's on her own. Oh, I *wish* it was me. She's going about. Now she's close-hauled.'

The girl had her back to them. Lynette noticed she wasn't wearing a life-jacket as she sailed on past Coronsay towards the open sea. They watched until she was out of sight. Then Toby gave a deep sigh.

Lynette got to her feet. 'We'd better get started on that hide-out or Uncle Alec will be back before we've finished. Or shall we eat first?'

There was no need to ask really. Toby was always hungry. He bounded down the hillside ahead of her, and then fell flat on his face. He sat up and rubbed his foot, looking aggrieved. 'I tripped over a hole,' he grumbled.

Lynette giggled. 'Something has to be sticking up before you can trip over it. Have some sense.'

'Well, I did. Here it is, and here's another . . . lots of little holes all over the place.' He stood up, looking indignant. 'They don't show up till you trip over them.'

'But . . .' Lynette began, and then thought better of it. She was no match for Toby in one of his argumentative moods.

The rolls and ham provided by their aunt tasted good in the salty air. As he ate Toby opened his sailing book and studied one of the diagrams with his forehead puckered in concentration. 'I've got to remember the difference between a jib sheet and a halyard,' he muttered with his mouth full.

By the time they reached the apple stage of the meal Lynette sprang up, anxious to get started on building the hide-out. Toby snapped his book shut, and ran with her over the soft sand to the cliffs.

There were plenty of loose boulders about to make a base for a rough sort of drystone wall where the cliff turned inwards.

'We'll need a lot of these,' Toby said as he heaved at a large rock. He staggered forward under its weight, tripped and dropped it heavily.

'Watch out!' Lynette cried as she sprang away.

Toby flexed his muscles. 'I can carry heavier ones than that.'

'We need small ones now to fill in the gaps.'

Toby busied himself climbing over rocks and jumping over rock pools to collect as many as he could. As she wedged them into place Lynette couldn't help thinking of the contrast of this quiet place with the busy parish that was going to be their new home. They had visited St George's once when Dad first knew he might be going there. Toby hadn't seemed to mind the thought of leaving all their friends in Cowthorpe where they had lived as long as she could remember, but she couldn't get used to the idea, however hard she tried.

'Dad feels it's the right decision, and so do I,' Mum had said. 'And it's perfect timing now you're eleven and finishing at junior school anyway, Lynette. Perhaps after the holiday in Scotland you'll feel better about it, love.'

Perhaps she would. She had forgotten about it yesterday in the excitement of arriving by train in Inverness, being met by Uncle Alec and being driven all the way to the remote cottage he and Aunt Ruth had moved into only last year. Now she must try to put it out of her mind for a while at least.

'We can make the roof from driftwood and pack lots of seaweed on top,' she said at last.

'Good camouflage,' said Toby. 'No one will ever see it.'

They dragged the wood across the beach, leaving

thick lines in the sand.

'We ought to have a name for it,' Lynette said when the seaweed was in place.

'Shanvara.'

'What made you think of that?'

Toby shrugged as he picked up a stone and skimmed it into the sea. 'How should I know?'

'Shanvara,' Lynette said slowly to try out how it sounded. 'Not bad. We'll call the hill Ben Vara.'

Toby bent to pick something up from the base of the cliff. 'A penknife,' he said in surprise.

The blades glinted in the sunshine as he opened it, and Lynette looked at it as if it was dynamite.

'Uncle Alec said no one came here,' she said indignantly. 'D'you think it's that girl in the sailing dinghy? She'll come here again and find Shanvara.'

'We'll fight her for it.' Toby turned the penknife over and studied the initials engraved on it. 'An E and F combined. It looks like silver. It could be loot from a burglary!'

Lynette shivered. 'It's eerie knowing someone's been here. It feels like we're being watched.' The sun didn't feel as hot now, and the hill, Ben Vara, looked dark. It was all a game to Toby, but life wasn't really a game. Suddenly Coronsay was a lonely, desolate place.

'We'll comb the island,' Toby said enthusiastically. 'If there's anyone else here we'll flush them out.'

He ran across the beach, but Lynette followed more slowly. She had wanted something to take her mind off her new home, and now she had it. But she didn't like this either. Toby was on the low headland now that jutted out into the channel between the island and mainland.

'Someone's been here all right,' he shouted. 'They've left their litter behind. And look, more holes. It's burglars hiding something.'

Suddenly Lynette thought of the boat sailing fast

away from shore. 'I wonder where that girl was going all on her own,' she said as she joined him and stood by his side gazing out at the empty sea.

Toby, with his nose near one of the holes, didn't answer. Lynette looked round in case there was anything else to be found, but there was nothing except the wild flowers in the grass among the rocky outcrops. She knew the names of some already, but some small mauve ones were strange to her. She'd bring her flower book with her next time . . . if there *was* a next time.

A gust of wind blew her loose hair across her face.

'I don't like it,' she said. 'I wish that girl would come back.'

They went back to the beach, and Lynette packed their things together hurriedly. Ben Vara looked darkly bleak behind her. She heard the sound of Uncle Alec's engine with relief.

Toby rushed into the water to meet him. 'Uncle Alec, there's a girl. She's gone right out to sea.'

Uncle Alec winked at Lynette. 'Swimming, was she?'

'Sailing close to the wind, and going really fast.'

'Well, laddie, we don't own the sea. She can do as she likes.'

'She wasn't wearing a life-jacket,' Lynette said anxiously as they both clambered aboard. 'We didn't notice her come back. I think something's happened to her.'

'Like capsizing,' Toby said with relish. 'Or getting hit unconscious by the boom.'

Their uncle laughed as he swung the tiller to head away from the beach.

'It's serious,' Lynette cried. 'I know it is.'

The sun was lower in the sky now, and the mountains were ringed in dusky shadows. Coronsay wasn't the beautiful exciting place they had thought at first. 'Let's go after her, Uncle Alec', she said, '*Please!*'

Chapter Two

'We haven't enough petrol to go much further,' Uncle Alec said.

He had taken the boat out a long way from the shore to give them a clear view for miles around. If the girl was out there they would see her. But no red sail was visible however much Lynette screwed up her eyes in an effort to see better. The girl had gone a long way. What would it feel like, she wondered with a little shiver, to spend all night alone on the deserted sea? Even the seagulls were silent.

'Oh *please* don't go back yet,' she begged. 'Can't we get the oars out and row for a bit?'

'No sense in that, lass. We'll go back and tell the coastguard. She's maybe gone further than she meant and the wind dropped, or . . .'

Lynette's throat was dry. 'Or what?'

She jumped as Toby let out a yell. 'Right over there, look! See that inlet further up the mainland? I'm sure I saw something red. It's the red sails.'

'Good lad,' Uncle Alec said as the engine surged and they went swiftly towards the shore.

Toby leaned right over the bows. 'The boat's in the inlet all right, pulled up on shore with the sails hanging loose. I can't see the girl, though.'

The engine sound changed as they got near and the boat slackened speed. Slowly it edged into the narrow channel between low rocky cliffs. Lynette kept her eyes on the water. One bump against those jagged submerged rocks and they would be in trouble.

Uncle Alec switched off the engine, and got the anchor ready to throw overboard. 'Too risky to go any further.'

Toby let out a shout that echoed among the dark cliffs. 'Where are you?'

There was no answer.

He leapt up. 'I'll swim ashore and look for her.' He stripped off his jersey and jeans to his swimming trunks beneath. He plunged in, and swam quickly.

Lynette watched anxiously as he stumbled ashore, and shook himself like a dog before scrambling over the boulders that lined the shore until he was out of sight.

To her relief he reappeared a moment later, a short stocky figure coming out from behind the rocks. 'I've seen her,' he shouted to them waving his arm. 'She's over there. I won't be long.'

For several moments there was silence. Lynette wondered what was taking Toby such a long time. She glanced at Uncle Alec and saw him gazing at the cliffs, a frown creasing his tanned forehead.

'Where do you think she came from?' she asked at last. 'Do you know her, Uncle?'

He turned to her, and a smile lit up his blue eyes. 'This late in the summer there aren't many holiday-makers about. But maybe the McClarens' caravan has been let.' He looked towards the shore again. 'Come on, laddie,' he murmured. 'We've waited long enough.'

Toby appeared again, right on cue. They could see that something was wrong by the way he was waving both arms and looking back over his shoulder.

'She won't come,' he called to them across the water. 'I've tried to make her, but she wants to stay where she is. She's hurt her ankle. She won't let me help her.'

'Wait there, Toby.' Uncle Alec's voice sounded confident. With one swift movement he had the anchor up and was reaching for an oar. 'There's no help for it. We'll have to go further in. Look out for rocks, Lynette. Shout out if we get too close.'

He had the oar out over the stern. Slowly they moved forward. When the anchor went down again Toby let out a cheer.

At once Uncle Alec was over the side, waist deep in water. He waded ashore, and then he and Toby vanished behind the rocks again.

They could only have been gone a few moments, but to Lynette waiting in the empty boat it seemed like hours before she heard voices and then saw Uncle Alec carrying the girl in his arms. Beside him Toby scrambled over the rocks, slipping every now and again in his haste to keep up.

Uncle Alec's face was stern. 'Float her boat off shore, Toby,' he said when they reached the water's edge. 'And be quick about it.'

From the motor boat Lynette watched in amazement as the girl tried hard to free herself.

'Any more nonsense, lass, and I'll tie your hands to the mast,' Uncle Alec said, tipping the girl into her dinghy and indicating to Toby that he should get in with her, too. Then he waded out from shore, propelling the dinghy in front of him until Lynette could lean out of the motorboat and hold it steady.

'The tow rope,' he ordered. 'Beneath the thwart there, Lynette, and be quick.'

Lynette found the rope, and her uncle tied it to the dinghy's mast. Then he got himself aboard his own boat. 'Climb over, too,' he told Toby.

Toby did as he was told, moving neatly from one boat to the other. His eyes were bright, and he smiled. The girl turned her back to them, holding her shoulders in a stiff line.

Lynette was relieved when Uncle Alec started his

engine and they moved slowly out of the inlet.

Toby, his teeth chattering, pulled on his clothes over his wet trunks. 'Her name's Rowena Havill,' he said. 'She told me that much before Uncle came. Did you see him carrying her like a baby? I thought he was going to drop her on those jagged rocks. Serve her right if he had.'

'Serve her right, why?'

'She made a real fuss. I can't see why she wanted to stay there on her own instead of being pleased we came to take her back.'

Lynette looked at the girl who now sat huddled in the stern of her sailing dinghy with one hand gripping the tiller. Rowena Havill, she thought, and then remembered the penknife they had found on the island. It didn't belong to the girl. The initials engraved on it were an E and an F, so it wasn't hers. So who else had been to Coronsay? She glanced back at Rowena who glared at her before turning her back in a very pointed way.

Lynette looked at Coronsay's silver beach as they passed between the island and the mainland on their way to the harbour. She couldn't see Shanvara because it was well disguised with its driftwood roof and the seaweed on top. Shanvara was their secret still, for a little while at least.

Two people stood on the jetty, a man with a boy of about Toby's age with a camera slung round his neck. The boy had the fairest hair Lynette had ever seen. He wasn't a bit like the girl, but was obviously her brother by the words he was shouting. 'It *is* Rowena, Dad. She's safe. The sail's down, but the boat's all right.'

The man could see that for himself, but the expression on his pale face was of fury rather than relief. He waited until Uncle Alec's boat nudged the jetty before telling his daughter exactly what he thought of her.

14

'She's injured her ankle,' Uncle Alec said at last as he helped the girl out onto dry land. 'It looks bad to me.'

Her father looked anxiously at Rowena, his anger gone now. 'How did it happen? Is it bad, Rowena?'

Uncle Alec indicated with a flick of his hand that Lynette and Toby should get out too. Then he pushed off the boat from the jetty and went to his mooring.

The colour was back in Mr Havill's cheeks by the time Uncle Alec had rowed himself ashore in his rubber dinghy. Rowena's father turned to thank him as he stepped out. 'But for you she'd have been missing all night.'

'It was my nephew Toby's sharp eyes that spied her,' Uncle Alec said gravely. 'Lynette, too, was responsible for us looking for her in the first place. You have them to thank.'

Rowena's brother was folding the sails now with Toby's help. Rowena stood by silently as they stowed the sails away in the sail bag.

Toby looked at Mr Havill, his eyes shining. 'We watched her sail past the island. It was great. I wished it was me going right out to sea like that.'

'Can you sail, lad?'

Toby shook his head, and sighed. 'I've got a book about sailing. I know about it in theory.'

'Like to learn?'

Toby almost dropped the sail bag in his excitement. '*Would* I?'

Mr Havill smiled, and rescued the sail bag. 'We'll have to arrange something. What about tomorrow?'

'That would be great!'

'Neil can give a hand too. All right, Neil?'

The fair haired boy nodded enthusiastically.

His father looked at Uncle Alec. 'Do you know anything about Roddy McClaren from the shop? We've got their caravan for two weeks. Would he stand by and

15

keep an eye on things if we can't be here with the children on other days? If Toby takes to sailing he'll want to do more of it, and Rowena and Neil would be glad of his company. Lynette's too. There's no reason why they shouldn't get together other days is there?'

Uncle Alec smiled. 'Aye, Roddy's a fine reliable lad. There's no one I'd trust as much as Roddy McClaren.'

Mr Havill looked relieved. 'That's settled then. Where shall we meet Lynette and Toby tomorrow?'

'Over on the island, maybe. It's as good a place as any for a sailing lesson.' Uncle Alec cocked an eyebrow at Toby who nodded eagerly.

'On Coronsay?' Lynette cried in dismay. But no one heard her except the girl, Rowena, who looked at her without saying anything. Toby was too busy making arrangements, his voice squeaky with excitement.

Lynette was silent as she walked up the road later at Uncle Alec's side. She thought of the girl, Rowena, who hadn't wanted them to bring her back. Rowena wouldn't take kindly to anyone learning to sail her boat, and especially not herself and Toby.

She swallowed hard, and looked back at Coronsay, dim now in the fading light. Toby wouldn't mind about Shanvara not being their secret any more now they had a chance to sail. But she felt very lonely. Everything was changing, and it was beginning to feel as if she wasn't only going to lose Shanvara but Toby too.

Chapter Three

'We're on a broad reach,' Mr Havill said. 'That means the wind is coming from one side of us.'

Toby nodded, his forehead creased in concentration. He thought hard of the diagram in his sailing book that showed the different points of sailing. He knew about a broad reach, of course, but he must think ahead and work out what to do when they changed course.

He had been studying his book hard while he and Lynette waited on the island beach for Rowena and Neil and their father to appear round the headland in their red-sailed dinghy. To his surprise the time had flown. Lynette had been content to climb about picking flowers, but he had more important things to go over and memorise. He had only listened with half an ear to Lynette talking about the caravan on the other side of the hill where the Havill family were staying. He could think only about their sailing dinghy. Who cared about a caravan, anyway? It was the boat that mattered!

'We'll practise going about,' Mr Havill said. 'It's a lightish wind so you won't need to come over to the other side, Toby. You and Neil balance each other. Ready about? Lee-oh.' He moved the tiller across. Neil let go of the jib sheet so that the small sail, the jib, hung down for a second.

Neil grinned at him, the sunshine glinting on his fair hair. 'Pull it in on your side, Toby.'

Toby did so, and he felt the jib tighten. He smiled,

liking the feeling that it was his action that had them moving ahead so well.

'All right?' Mr Havill asked. 'The wind's just right for beginners. You'd have to move across smartish in a stronger wind or you'd have the boat over. We'll practise some running now with the wind astern.'

He moved the tiller across slightly. Both sails now were well out on opposite sides of the boat. They moved along silently, and the land behind them slipped away. They went past the harbour entrance and changed to a broad reach.

'The wind's different today,' Toby said. 'Rowena was close-hauled yesterday when she came this way. The sails were pulled in really tight.'

Neil and his father exchanged glances. 'Lucky for her you were watching,' Mr Havill said grimly. 'Ready about? Lee-oh.'

'Broad reach again,' Toby murmured as they came round to head back the way they had come with the wind on one side of them again.

Mr Havill smiled in approval. 'You're coming on,' he said, and Toby flushed with pleasure.

'Can we go right round the island, Dad?' Neil asked.

His father glanced at his watch. 'Not today. More sailing tomorrow if you like, Toby, but I promised to get back quickly today.'

'But not us, Dad. We'll sail with you to the harbour, and then go back to Coronsay on our own.'

'Uncle Alec will bring us back,' Toby said as he let the jib sheet out a fraction. 'It's easy towing another boat.'

They neared the harbour entrance.

'We'll have to tack now because we're changing direction and heading into the wind,' Neil said.

Both sails were pulled in tightly, and the boat heeled a little as they bore round.

'If I let you go back to Coronsay on your own will

you promise not to do any more sailing after that?' his father said. 'Leave that for tomorrow when Roddy McClaren's with you.'

Neil nodded enthusiastically, grinning at Toby. 'Thanks, Dad.'

They entered the harbour. Minutes later Mr Havill brought the boat gently towards the jetty.

Neil took the tiller as his father got out. He shook his mop of fair hair away from his face as they set off again. He looked happy and confident. 'This is great.'

Toby was wishing they could go on for ever. He couldn't, even now, really believe his luck. And tomorrow too! He grinned at Neil who was pulling in the main sheet.

'I don't get the chance much to helm when Rowena's around,' Neil said.

They changed direction several times. Neil gave the orders sharply, saying 'Ready about? Lee-oh,' each time. Toby knew exactly what to do.

'Just practising,' said Neil as they went about again.

On the island beach Lynette watched the small red-sailed boat come round the headland. She liked the name she had seen on the stern as Mr Havill and the boys sailed out of the harbour for Toby's first lesson. '*Seaspray*,' she murmured to herself. Yes, it was just right. Shanvara was a good name for the shelter too. Should they tell Neil and Rowena about it before they discovered it for themselves?

Rowena hadn't been at all pleased to be helped into Uncle Alec's boat to be brought to the island to wait for the lesson to finish. She hadn't spoken once since Uncle Alec marooned them here on Coronsay.

Now, Lynette glanced doubtfully at Rowena sitting hunched on a rock a little distance away. From the beginning there was no mistaking that she wanted nothing to do with any of them. Lynette had tried to be friendly at first, but had then given it up as a bad job and wandered off up the hill to watch the boys and Mr Havill in *Seaspray*. She had seen them drop Neil's father off at the jetty and then come sailing back in a slow zig-zagging way. Now they were nearing Coronsay.

She looked at Rowena again. It was a bad feeling being disliked. All they had done, she and Toby and Uncle Alec, was to offer help when it was needed. Had it been herself instead of Rowena she would have been grateful. Love your neighbour as yourself, she thought, and that's what they had done.

Rowena was tall with dark curly hair and brown eyes. She looked as if she would be good at things, too. Anyone could like *her* if she was nice to them, so why shouldn't she like herself? And here she was on holiday with her family, and they had their own sailing dinghy. Toby would think that no one could possibly be happier!

Lynette looked out at *Seaspray* again, and then gasped. A motor boat had come from nowhere, and they were going to collide at speed! She heard Neil's frantic yell and the creak as the boom swung across. *Seaspray* rocked and changed direction just in time. The other boat vanished behind the headland. It had happened so quickly that Lynette's legs felt like jelly as she ran into the water to meet them.

'Did you see that?' Toby cried as he swung his legs over *Seaspray*'s side and leapt out into shallow water. 'He nearly came into us.'

She was relieved to see that he was indignant rather than frightened. Not that a near collision would put him off learning to sail. Nothing would.

Rowena hobbled down to them as they lifted the boat clear of the water. 'What were you playing at, Neil?' she demanded. 'You're so dismal at helming.'

'The boat shouldn't have been there,' Toby said. 'It's Sunday. Uncle Alec said no boats are about on a Sunday.'

Rowena looked scornful. 'That's no excuse. It's the crew's job to keep a look-out. Why didn't you tell him?'

Neil flicked back his fair hair. '*We* were under sail, not him. He should have kept away. I wish I'd had my camera with me.'

'The motor boat came so suddenly,' Lynette objected. 'It wasn't Toby's fault.'

Toby looked uncomfortable. 'I didn't see it until it was too late.'

Rowena, ignoring them, glared at her brother. 'You were messing about, Neil.'

He grinned. 'The man had a bit of a shock too. His fault, not ours.'

'You should have more sense.'

'Like you had yesterday?' he retorted. 'Who went too far and got becalmed when the wind dropped? Who landed in a lonely place, and then tripped and hurt her ankle? Who knew she'd been stupid but wouldn't admit it?'

Rowena pushed her dark hair back behind her ears with an angry gesture. Her face had whitened, and Lynette looked at her in alarm. Perhaps her ankle, tightly bandaged after her visit to the doctor, was hurting. Things were getting out of hand. Everything was different now, and it wasn't just because Rowena was around. Lynette wondered if the motorboat had tried to collide with *Seaspray* on purpose.

'We're going to light a fire and cook the mackerel we brought with us,' she said quickly.

'I'm starving,' Toby said.

'Me too.' Neil removed his life-jacket and threw it into the boat.

Toby made no move to take his off. He liked wearing it even though its bulkiness restricted his movements. 'Have you got the dry wood out of *Shanvara*?' he asked.

Lynette froze. Toby had forgotten it was a secret!

Neil looked interested. '*Shanvara* . . . what's that?'

There was silence. What could she do? It was only a home-made hide-out after all. What did it matter if Rowena made fun of it? The Havills had been generous about sharing their boat, so how could she make a fuss about sharing Shanvara?

'Come on,' she said. 'We'll show you.'

They went across the beach, Toby still in the orange life-jacket, and Rowena limping along behind looking disdainfully at the cliffs and rocks.

Neil exclaimed in delight when he saw the entrance to Shanvara. He examined the seaweed roof, and then went inside.

Lynette glanced anxiously at Rowena. 'Are you coming in too? There's lots to show you . . .'

But Rowena didn't answer.

Neil's muffled voice came from deep inside. 'There's even somewhere to keep your things. Did it take long to make?'

Toby tried to go in too, but his life-jacket got stuck in the entrance.

Lynette giggled. 'It's no good. You'll have to take it off.'

Toby tried again, but had to give up and remove the bulky life-jacket. He threw it on the sand in disgust, and Lynette was still smiling as she followed him inside.

There was plenty of room for the three of them, and for Rowena too, if she had wanted to come.

Neil pushed aside some of the seaweed so he could get a good view of the beach. 'It's great,' he said. 'You could hide here for ever. No one would guess where you were.'

Lynette looked out too, and saw Rowena limping across the beach carrying the discarded life-jacket. She put it with the other one in *Seaspray* and then stood leaning on the boat with her back to them. She stayed there on her own all the time they were lighting the fire on the sand and collecting more driftwood.

Tongues of flame spluttered on the tarry wood which was so dry there was no smoke, only a hot shimmer of air above the flames. Neil, kneeling by it with his fair head bent, fed it wood very carefully. Lynette cut the bones out of the mackerel, and then threw the remains to a horde of greedy seagulls whose clamour might have been heard on the mainland.

'You're lucky being allowed to light a fire,' Neil said, sitting back on his heels.

Toby got the water container out of the rucksack and filled the kettle. 'It's safe enough on the sand. Uncle Alec always did it when he was a boy, so he lets us.'

The fish sizzled in the frying pan. Lynette's face was burning and she moved back a little to butter the rolls in comfort. Neil got out their contribution of apples and biscuits, and then looked across at his sister. 'Come on Rowena, it's ready.'

At first it didn't look as if she was going to come. Then she moved slowly across the sand towards them, and sat down in silence.

'This is the best meal I've ever had,' said Neil as he started eating. 'Let's do it every day.'

Toby took a large mouthful of bap, and grinned at him. The sun was hot on his face. A slight breeze stirred *Seaspray*'s sails.

Neil leapt up. 'I'd better get the mainsail down.'

Toby ran with him to help. Lynette watched him getting in the way, but Neil didn't seem to mind. She turned to Rowena, and hesitated. There seemed nothing to say to her, but she wanted to be friendly. At once the boys came hurtling back for more food and the chance was lost.

'Who do you think was in that boat?' Toby said with his mouth full. 'That penknife could have been his.'

Neil stopped eating. 'What penknife?'

Lynette had forgotten about it. She felt in the pocket of her jeans for it. 'This one.'

'We found it near Shanvara yesterday,' Toby said. 'Then we found lots of small holes on the hill.'

Neil took the penknife from Lynette. 'It looks like silver. What will you do with it?'

Toby shrugged. 'I don't know if there's a policeman in Butallie.'

Neil handed the penknife back, and Lynette replaced it in her pocket. 'Roddy'll know. Roddy McClaren. He'll be here tomorrow. Do you know him?'

'His mother has the shop in Butallie,' said Lynette. 'You've got their caravan, haven't you? We've seen Roddy, in his bush hat. Uncle Alec says he sleeps in it.' She handed Neil one of the two cups of cocoa she had made. 'We'll have to take turns. I'll bring more cups tomorrow and keep them in Shanvara.'

The boys were still eating, and there was silence for a moment. Then Toby said, 'We were surprised to find the penknife. Uncle Alec said no one ever came here. He said no one used the boats in the harbour on Sundays either.'

'So he doesn't know what he's talking about,' Rowena said. She got up and moved across the beach where she sat down with her hands clasped round her knees staring out across the water.

Neil sipped his cocoa. 'Don't take any notice of her. I don't. She's been like this ever since . . . I mean, don't take any notice.'

Toby took a huge bite from his apple. 'I bet there's a connection between the man in the motor boat and Coronsay. Perhaps he's been here already today. Let's look for more holes. Coming?' Leaping up, he hurled his apple core into the sea where a waiting seagull swooped on it.

'Wait,' Lynette cried. 'Let's clear up first.'

But the boys were off. She followed them as soon as she had scraped all the bits into the fire, and rinsed the frying pan and cups with the water left in the kettle.

24

Toby gave a yell from the low headland. 'Someone's been here since yesterday. Come and look.'

She ran across. The holes were still there, and near them three plastic cups. A soaked newspaper lay on the ground. Matches had spilled out of a sodden box, and a piece of polythene sheeting was stuck fast to a projecting rock.

Neil kicked at it in disgust. 'What a mess!'

'I won't let them spoil Coronsay,' Lynette said indignantly as she started to pick up the cups and matches.

'Wait a minute,' said Neil. 'I'll take a photo as evidence.' He ran back to the beach to get his camera out of the food bag. It didn't take long to photograph the rubbish and the holes in the ground, too.

'That's great,' he said as he stood upright and put the camera back in its case. 'But don't tell Rowena. She thinks I waste my films.'

Lynette smiled as she rammed all the rubbish together to leave in a neat heap to be collected on their way back to the beach. She would have photographed the mackerel being cooked, and the four of them sitting near the fire.

As they climbed the hill to inspect the rest of the holes Toby had found yesterday she looked for more evidence that someone had been before them and to her relief found none.

'There aren't any more holes either,' Toby said in disappointment. 'Perhaps it's some animal after all.'

Neil's fair hair flopped over his face as he bent to look. 'But what animal makes holes like that?'

None of them knew, and they argued about it as they went down the hill to tidy their lunch things away in Shanvara. Toby scuffed out the ashes of the fire to spread them around before covering them with sand. Still Rowena didn't move.

When it was time to go Neil gave a happy sigh. 'We'll be able to do a bit of fishing tomorrow when Roddy

McClaren's here. Dad thinks we'll be safe enough with Roddy. Coronsay's a perfect place.'

Perfect? Lynette glanced at Rowena sitting with her back hunched, gazing out to sea. Was it really perfect when someone else's rubbish littered the ground, and when someone made those holes all over the place and dropped a penknife they might return to find? But worst of all was the silent Rowena, who was plainly hating every minute.

Chapter Four

'There's someone coming!' Toby hissed. At once he pulled Lynette inside Shanvara, and then pushed aside some of the seaweed on the roof so they could see out.

They had come early to Coronsay today because Uncle Alec had some business to see to in Inverness and Aunt Ruth was going with him to do some shopping.

'You'll be all right with Roddy McClaren there,' he had said with confidence. Mr Havill's arranged for him to keep his eye on Neil and Rowena, and on you too. Aye, Roddy's a good lad.'

Toby winked at Lynette. 'But what if the hole-makers come? We told you about them, remember?'

Uncle Alec, catching sight of the wink, laughed in his deep-throated way. 'Get them to dig some holes over here in my garden, lad. It needs a bit of attention.'

'Those holes are all over the place on Coronsay,' Lynette said seriously. 'Why there, Uncle Alec? What are they doing?'

'It's a free world, lass. Anyone can go to Coronsay.'

'I know, but . . .'

Her uncle laughed again, and ruffled Toby's hair as he got up from the breakfast table.

It was no use saying any more about it, but as they waited on Coronsay for Roddy and the others, Lynette couldn't help wondering if whoever made those holes would come again today.

And now it seemed that they had. Lynette pulled

aside some more of the roofing seaweed, and, her heart thumping, saw a strange boat moored a short distance off-shore. Two people waded to the beach, and set off towards the headland.

'Ordinary holidaymakers would stay on the beach,' she whispered. 'Or at least dump their picnic things there before exploring the island.'

'They aren't holidaymakers. I know they're not.' Toby's voice trembled with excitement.

The man had a dark beard, and wore a green jersey, and jeans tucked into high sea boots. He turned as he reached the low headland, and as he bent to point out something to the woman a flicker of sunlight reflected off his rimless glasses. The woman's jeans were wet below the knee, and she was wearing trainers. If it hadn't been for her long fair hair she would have been almost invisible against the dark heathery ground in her brown anorak.

'That's where the rubbish was left,' Toby whispered.

Lynette moved her head forward for a better look. 'What are they doing?'

'Brown Anorak's giving him something. I can't quite see . . .'

The man and woman were standing upright now, and moving away out of sight.

'I bet they've gone up the hill,' Toby said into Lynette's right ear. 'I'm gong to see.'

'No, no, wait! They might come back and see us.'

She could sense Toby's suppressed excitement, but he remained still. It seemed ages before they saw them again, but only a few minutes had passed.

'She's carrying something,' Lynette murmured. She could feel Toby's breath on her right cheek as he craned forward to look out on her side.

The two people walked down the beach and waded into the water. They clambered aboard their boat, and the engine started with a roar.

Lynette held on to Toby. 'We'll give them time to get right away.'

They waited until the boat had gone, and then three slow minutes more, before running to the low headland.

'Look, Lynette, they've made more holes. I'm certain they have,' Toby said.

She bent to look, but before she could say anything Toby was off up the hill. Then he was down on his knees crawling among the rocks and heather. 'They've dug things up,' he shouted. 'The earth's loose and black.'

She went up to him to look, and knelt down too. 'Plants . . . or earth samples?'

'But why?' There was a black smudge on Toby's nose, and as he rubbed his hand across his face there were more.

Lynette laughed as she got out a tissue and handed it to him. 'You've got a mucky face. Better clean it off before the others come.'

Toby stood up, and rubbed his face hard. There was no sign of the boat in the small harbour on the other side of the water, but a red-sailed dinghy and another motor boat with one person in it were coming out of it now. He gave a triumphant shout. 'They're coming. The others are coming!'

They were both breathless as they ran down to the water's edge.

'They're having to tack,' Toby said as they watched *Seaspray* zig-zagging towards the beach.

Roddy McClaren was standing in the stern of his fishing boat, *Shona*, as it came gently towards them. The tiller was held lightly in one hand, and his khaki bush hat was on his head. He was wearing sea boots like the man they had seen, and his grey shirt was open at the neck. He turned the tiller a little, cut the engine and dropped the anchor overboard. Then he swung himself over the side, and waded ashore carrying a khaki bag over one shoulder.

'You're the Craigs,' he stated rather than asked as he placed his bag on the sand at his feet.

Lynette nodded. She knew he was at least seventeen, and she felt slightly awkward. But *Seaspray* was coming now, moving directly into the wind to slow her down. Neil sprang out at once, and held the boat steady with Toby's help so that Rowena could get out too.

'We saw them,' Toby burst out as they lifted *Seaspray* onto the sand. 'Just now. They came. We saw them . . . a man and a woman. They came back here, and . . .'

'What are you on about?' Rowena asked scornfully. 'I didn't know you owned the island.' She threw him a look of contempt as she limped away from the water and stood by Roddy who was busy opening his bag and taking out some fishing reels.

'What's that for?' Neil asked. He had looked interested in Toby's news for a moment, but then was side-tracked by what Roddy was doing.

'Don't you want to know?' Toby cried. 'Those people we told you about . . . they weren't here long, and then they went off in their boat. Did you see them?'

'We saw no one,' Roddy said, straightening.

Neil's face brightened. 'We could go and look for them, couldn't we? I've got my camera. Can we, Roddy, in your boat? We can fish at the same time.'

'Aye, we'll catch our own food today, right enough,' Roddy said. 'Plenty of mackerel for the catching. No harm if we take a trip round the island in *Shona* too.'

'All of us?' Toby asked eagerly. He was looking at Roddy with a reverent expression on his face.

'Why not?' Roddy's eyes were very blue and the expression in them direct.

Toby's gaze followed him as he pulled out a polythene container and opened it. Inside were cut up remains of fish and some bread.

'Is that for bait?' asked Neil.

Roddy nodded as he replaced the lid. 'Aye, and plenty for all.'

'Not me,' said Rowena. 'I'm sailing, not fishing.'

The others looked at Roddy expectantly. He was older than they were, and there was something else about him too that seemed to make him a natural leader.

He looked up at the sky, and frowned slightly. 'You'll need someone with you.'

'Not me,' said Neil.

'Toby?'

'He can go with you,' Rowena said. 'I'm going sailing with Lynette.'

Lynette was surprised. 'Me?'

Rowena looked at her, a glint of a threat in her dark eyes. 'Dad said I had to teach you to sail, and that's what I'm going to do. Not afraid, are you?'

She sounded triumphant and Lynette knew she was testing her. She stood up straight, and stared back at Rowena. 'No, I'm not afraid,' she said, but her heart was thumping. She picked up the life-jacket Neil had thrown down, glad that she was wearing shorts today.

The water felt cold as she helped the boys get *Seaspray* into the water, and she couldn't help a slight shudder as she got in and sat down. She hoped that Rowena, busy with the rudder, didn't notice.

It was all right at first with the wind dead astern, but Lynette knew that they would have to gybe soon. Toby had told her about the boom swinging across from one side of the boat to the other in order to change direction when the wind was behind you.

'Ready to gybe?' Rowena said suddenly. 'Gybe-oh.' She wrenched the tiller over, and the boom cracked across the boat. Then she leaned forward to push down the centreboard, and hauled in the mainsheet.

Lynette gasped as *Seaspray* heeled over and gathered speed.

'Not scared are you?' Rowena shouted.

' 'Course not,' said Lynette, white-lipped.

'Ready about? Lee-oh. Change sides and be quick about it.'

Lynette was across in a flash, and grabbed the jib sheet with shaking hands.

'Hurry,' Rowena snapped. 'You'll have us over.'

Then it was time to go about once more, and they both leaned out over the side to balance the boat again.

'This is fun!' Rowena cried.

It seemed to Lynette that they were going on for miles, far out past Coronsay. 'We're going too far,' she shouted desperately.

But Rowena only laughed.

Lynette gritted her teeth, and hung on to the jib with aching fingers. 'We ought to go back to the others,' she gasped after a while.

Rowena grinned. 'Don't be dismal. I wouldn't miss this for anything. Ready about? Lee-oh.'

They were round. The jib flapped until Lynette grabbed the sheet on the other side and pulled in hard. Backwards and forwards they went, until she was sure the skin on her hands was worn right away. She dared not turn her head to see where the others were, but did as she was ordered as fast as she could.

Rowena, still exultant, was enjoying every minute. Toby would have been in his element, loving it all.

'Please God, stop me being afraid,' Lynette whispered desperately. She didn't know if she spoke aloud or not, only that she needed help to cope with it all even though they were now going back towards the beach.

The constant noise of the sea slapping against the bows rang in her ears, but the sudden deafening crack when it came took her completely by surprise. The boat lurched violently, and water began to pour in.

Without thinking, Lynette leapt into the middle of

the boat, and clung to the centreboard case as *Seaspray* swung into the wind. For an incredible moment she saw another boat with the man and woman she had seen earlier in it, and then it was gone again behind *Seaspray*'s flapping sails.

'Find the bailer,' Rowena spluttered, almost speechless with rage. 'Get bailing.'

Lynette did as she was told, but it seemed to make no difference to the water in the boat. Rowena grabbed the bailer from her angrily, and the water flew over the side like a fountain. Then she threw it back to Lynette, got the paddle out and used it furiously to propel them along until there was a soft bump. To find themselves so near the beach gave Lynette a jolt of relieved surprise. She was out at the same time as Rowena and helping her haul the boat clear.

Now they were safe on land her legs began to tremble, and she took a deep gasp of air. Was it her fault that something had gone wrong?

Rowena was glaring out to sea, muttering to herself, and Lynette didn't dare ask her. There was no sign of any other boat, not even *Shona*. A feeling of loneliness swept over her.

Suddenly Rowena got hold of *Seaspray*'s bow and heaved it up so that streams of water poured out at the stern. Lynette moved to help her, and together they waited until it had all gone. Then, carefully, they lowered the boat on to the sand again.

Now Lynette saw the jagged gash on one side. She gazed at it in horror. Rowena's face had turned a dark red, and she was scowling.

'It was deliberate. Did you see them? Came up from nowhere, far too close, and forced us onto the rocks. Just let me get at them!'

'But you can't,' Lynette cried in alarm.

'I know that, stupid.'

Relieved that it wasn't her fault, Lynette let it pass.

She unzipped her life-jacket and took it off, feeling much more like herself.

'The boys aren't here either, just when we need them,' Rowena raged. 'It's too dismal.' She began to lower the mainsail, working quickly so that it was down and being detached before Lynette could offer to help. She stood silently and watched as Rowena dealt with the jib.

'We'll fold them and get them in the sail bag,' Rowena said when she was ready. 'Fetch it . . . it's over there.'

She seemed more approachable now that she was doing something.

'I'm sorry it happened,' Lynette dared to say when she got back with the bag. 'I thought it was me . . . doing something wrong, I mean.'

Rowena made no reply until the sails were away and she was drawing tight the string at the top. She put the bag down, and threw herself down on the sand and sat with her arms round her knees.

Lynette sat down too. Her legs still felt weak and her arms ached. She was glad it was over, even in this way. Who knew how far she would have been taken otherwise?

Now the crisis was over, Rowena's inner fury seemed to have evaporated. Encouraged, Lynette began to tell her about Toby's sailing book and the way he had come out with bits of information she had tried to remember and use.

'The wind was too strong for a beginner,' Rowena said grudgingly.

Lynette smiled. It was almost an apology. 'There was so much noise . . . in the sails, and the sea hitting the bows.'

'Your lips were moving. I saw them.'

'That's because I was praying.'

'*Praying?*'

'I always ask God for help when I'm worried. He's

always with me, you see. So that's what I was doing . . .
talking to him.'

She tensed, waiting for Rowena's scorn. Saying this
was even harder than trusting herself with Rowena in
the boat. There was silence for a moment.

Then a distant seagull called. Lynette looked round
and saw *Shona* far out, moving slowly towards them.
Toby and Neil seemed engrossed in their fishing lines.
So *they* hadn't seen anything . . .

'And what did you pray?' Rowena asked at length.

'I asked God to help me not to be afraid.'

Rowena looked at her incredulously. 'Afraid? Who
could be afraid? It was terrific.'

'Not for me,' Lynette said firmly. 'We're different,
that's all.'

Rowena scowled, and a dark flush covered her face.
It was plain she was upset, but too deeply, surely, for
such a simple remark? There was something odd here.
Lynette tried to think of something helpful to say, but
Rowena turned her back on her and walked away across
the beach.

Chapter Five

Rowena was back again by the time the boys returned in *Shona*. They all stared at *Seaspray*. The dinghy lay on one side on the beach with the jagged tear side uppermost.

Roddy took off his bush hat, and scratched his head. 'It's bad, right enough.'

Toby's face was red with indignation. 'What are we going to *do*?' He could hardly contain himself at Roddy's calm manner as the older boy looked thoughtfully at the damage.

Neil looked uncomfortable. 'Dad won't trust us again if he sees this. Are you sure that's what happened Rowena? You weren't just playing about?'

His sister's face darkened, but before she could retort Lynette said quickly, 'One minute they were there. The next they weren't. It happened so quickly, but it wasn't Rowena's fault.'

Roddy put his hat back on. 'Aye, it'll have been a shock.'

'But can't we do something?' Toby asked impatiently.

'We'll go after them of course, in *Shona*. What are we waiting for?' Already Rowena was ankle deep in the sea.

Roddy followed her. 'No way! We'll head for the mainland. Get ready to launch *Seaspray*, you three,' he shouted back to them. 'I've got a tow rope aboard.'

Toby watched open-mouthed, as Roddy overtook

Rowena and sprang into his boat. He leant over and helped her aboard, before fishing out a rope and returning with it to the others.

'But why are we taking *Seaspray*?' Toby asked as he caught hold of the dinghy with the others and lifted it into the water.

Roddy was on the side of the gash, making sure he held it high until the other three got in on the other side. They were low in the water, and Lynette couldn't help a little gasp as some came over the side.

Neil moved into the centre a little for a better balance. 'Roddy's right. We've got to get repairs done. He may know someone.'

'But we can't chase the Rammers like this,' Toby said indignantly. 'They'll be miles away by now.'

Lynette shuddered. 'A good thing too. What would you do if we caught them up?'

'They might come back and smash *Seaspray* if we went off in *Shona*,' Lynette pointed out as they began moving slowly away.

Toby was silent, thinking about it.

Neil made sure the gash stayed well above the water line by moving to keep his side of the boat low in the water. No one said anything as they went slowly round the headland.

There was no sign of anyone as Roddy took them carefully across the strip of water and along the coast of the mainland to where the few houses of Butallie slumbered in the morning sunshine. It was incredible how the wind had dropped. Here near the shore the water was like glass, and the reflections of the houses and the brown salty seaweed beneath the surface hardly stirred.

As they neared the jetty, Roddy cut off his engine and brought *Shona* gently alongside so that the three in *Seaspray* could lean over to the wooden structure and propel themselves along behind. It was a matter of moments to secure both boats, and clamber out.

'We'll need to manoeuvre *Seaspray* round and then paddle in to lift her out of the water,' Roddy said.

Toby was first into the water, sliding a little on the slimy stones. When they had got the dinghy out of the water he turned an indignant face to Roddy. 'Those people who came to Coronsay . . . *they* must have done it. We saw them come, didn't we Lynette? Rammers is a good name for them.'

'I think . . . I'm *sure* they're the same people we saw on Coronsay,' Lynette said.

'We think they were digging things up.'

Roddy coiled up the tow rope and put it in *Shona*. 'Where did they come from? Butallie?'

'We didn't see where they went,' said Lynette. 'We stayed hidden. A man with a beard and glasses, and a woman in a brown anorak. They didn't know we were there.'

Roddy stood up straight, a glint in his eyes. 'Digging something up, you said?'

'It looked like it,' said Lynette. 'Plants perhaps, or earth samples? I couldn't identify a little mauve flower I saw yesterday. Do you think it was that? It might be rare.'

'It'll be earth samples,' said Neil. 'They wouldn't go to all that trouble for a *flower*.'

'The earth on Coronsay, the heather, the plants, belong there.' Roddy's voice was like steel. 'No one takes them from me.'

'But Coronsay's not yours,' Rowena pointed out.

He rounded on her fiercely. 'It's mine because I love it.'

There was a moment's tense silence. Then Rowena shrugged. 'What about *Seaspray*?' she said. 'Who's going to do the repairs before Dad sees it?'

'Aye.' Roddy seemed to relax. 'I've a place behind the shop. No problem, but it'll take time, right enough.'

Roddy's workshop was a large outhouse equipped with a work bench that looked well-used. Lynette wrinkled her nose at the smell of sawdust and diesel oil as they went in. Neil and Toby pulled *Seaspray* in after them on Roddy's boat trolley.

Toby looked round admiringly. 'Is it really your own place, Roddy? It's great.'

Roddy looked pleased. 'It's mine now. It used to be Dad's. He did some fine work here. He taught me a lot.'

'About mending boats?'

'Fishing, too. And how best to study.'

Toby was surprised. 'Study?'

'I'm wanting to go in for engineering.' Roddy's eyes followed Neil and Lynette as they wandered round looking at the coils of rope and the baskets hanging from the roof at the far side. As they came back he ran his fingers over the tear in the boat.

'How long will it take?' asked Toby.

'There's no telling till I start.'

'I'm hungry,' said Neil. 'When are we going to eat?'

Cooking the mackerel the boys had caught over an open fire wouldn't do, so Rowena got out the bag with the Havills' food from where it had been stuffed right into the bows of their dinghy, while Neil ran down to the jetty to bring Roddy's bag from *Shona*. He had the bucket of fish, too, which he placed in a dark corner.

'Our things are still in Shanvara,' Lynette said regretfully.

'We've got plenty for us all,' said Neil.

Roddy, intent on what he was doing, shook his head when he was offered a sandwich. The others sat on the dusty floor to eat.

Afterwards they left him hard at work, and went to the shop for ice-creams. Toby pushed open the door and set the bell jangling. It didn't stop until they were all inside and the door closed.

Mrs McClaren came out from a back room, rubbing her floury hands. 'Is it ices you're wanting?' she asked in her soft voice. She had a smile that lit up her round face and made her seem almost as young as Roddy. As she scooped generous portions of ice-cream to ram down hard in the cornets she asked about the fishing.

'We caught lots of mackerel,' Toby boasted. 'You should see them in the bucket in the workshop. I got three.'

'You'll be needing to have them cooked for you then,' Mrs McClaren said. 'Maybe for tea?'

Lynette smiled. 'Thank you. That would be great!'

Roddy's mother smiled at Toby. 'I'll have them ready for you if you get them for me.'

Toby was off at once. A black cat sidled round the door, and Rowena bent to stroke him. 'He's lovely What's his name?'

'That's Nimrod.' Mrs McClaren held out the last of the ices to Lynette to hold. 'Likes a bit of hunting, the naughty boy. He's been off somewhere now, just look at him.'

He was loving the fuss Rowena was making of him, and she picked him up as they went out of the shop to sit on the wall to eat their ice-creams. When she had finished hers she sat with him on her lap, smoothing his fur with her long fingers. A sudden rustling in the grass alerted him at once, and he was off before she could stop him.

Back inside the workshop Roddy was still busy. He had sawn a square piece out of the side to get rid of the jagged tear, and was bevelling the edges to forty-five degrees as they went in.

Rowena scowled. 'What a dismal mess you've made of it, Roddy. Dad'll be livid.'

Roddy took no notice, but Neil rounded on her. 'Leave him alone, can't you? What do you know about it?'

'More than you do anyway.'

They stood glaring at each other while Roddy reached for a piece of wood he had ready, and began to file it. Toby shuffled his feet, while Lynette felt awkward at the speed a row between the two of them seemed to be blowing up.

Neil flushed, and glared at his sister. Rowena looked as if she was going to hit him. Then she turned and ran.

'Let her go,' Neil said.

For a moment Lynette hesitated before going to the open door and looking out. Rowena was going as fast as she could with her bad ankle up the hill behind the shop. Lynette stood in the doorway, wondering what to do. Then she followed her.

She found Rowena just over the brow of the hill, lying face downwards in the heather. She sat down beside her, and waited.

At last Rowena sat up, looking wild-eyed and with her dark hair in a mess. She pushed it back impatiently. 'What are you doing here?' She snatched at a stalk of heather and began pulling off the flowers to trickle through her fingers.

'It's odd that no two stalks of heather are exactly alike,' said Lynette.

'What?'

'Everyone's different. Like people are different from each other.' Too late she remembered Rowena's reaction yesterday when being different was mentioned.

'It's all right for *you* being different,' Rowena cried passionately. 'But I don't *want* to be different!'

'Why not?'

But Rowena didn't reply. 'Your dad's a vicar, isn't he?' she asked instead. 'It's easy for you.'

'No it isn't,' Lynette said hotly. Instantly she thought of where her parents were at this very minute . . . in a place she dreaded living and where they would be

41

moving almost as soon as they went home from staying with Uncle Alec and Aunt Ruth. Perhaps she ought to think about it more, and get properly used to the idea.

She knew that Rowena was challenging her, and she must take it up even though she suspected that whatever she said would be thrown back in her face.

'No one can *tell* you to love God,' she said after a while. 'You must want to do it for yourself.' Dad had said it was a challenge going to a new place like Dankford. But it meant leaving all her friends, and the things she liked doing. So, still feeling like this, how was she going to be able to help Rowena?

Rowena pulled at a stalk of heather which broke off in her hand. She scowled. 'Anyway you can shut up about people being different. It's boring.' She turned her back, and sat with her shoulders hunched. 'Can't you see I want to be alone?'

Lynette got awkwardly to her feet and went back down the hill, feeling useless. Toby was still in the workshop helping Roddy when she looked in.

'Neil's gone down to the jetty,' he told her.

The sun shone briefly, highlighting Neil's fair hair, as she walked down to join him. She sat on a large stone, and watched him skimming pebbles in the clear water. He grinned cheerfully as his pebble did five hops before sinking down.

No one would know he had a sister like Rowena, she thought. She wondered what it was like staying in a caravan with her in her awkward mood. Maybe Neil was extra nice to make up for it.

'Where's your camera?' she asked. 'I thought you'd be taking photos of the gash in the boat.'

Neil paused in his skimming, and turned to her in surprise. 'You must be joking! If Mum saw a photo of the damage she'd go mad with worry, and Dad would accuse Rowena of having done it on purpose. Then Mum would be in tears and she and Rowena would have one of their rows. Roddy's doing a great job on the boat. I'll take the photo when it's done.'

'But won't it show?'

'Not when Roddy's finished.'

Several people wandered past. Some went into the shop and came out with ice-creams. One man came along on his own, an elderly grey-haired man walking with a stick and with a pair of binoculars slung round his neck.

'I've seen him before,' Neil whispered. 'He was in the boat we nearly collided with on Sunday.'

Lynette turned to look, and as she did so the man seemed to notice them. He hesitated, and then came across slowly.

Chapter Six

The man smiled at them. 'On holiday?'

Lynette let out the long breath she was holding, and nodded.

'Are you on holiday too?' Neil asked boldly.

'Not quite like you, I'm afraid.' He gazed at them intently as if trying to discover everything about them just by looking. His tanned face was heavily lined on the forehead and round his eyes. As he moved slightly his stick caught against a stone which rolled away. He looked down at it in surprise, and when he looked up again he was smiling.

'We're staying in the McClarens' caravan,' said Neil. 'The one near the disused croft house.'

'You're staying there, are you? A fine place for a holiday. Interested in wildlife, are you? Seen anything of interest?'

Neil hesitated. Lynette, afraid he would tell this stranger too much too soon, hastily cleared her throat as she tried to think of something to say. He looked at her enquiringly, and she felt herself flush. 'Ah, then you know Roddy?' he said. 'A fine boy. I knew his father. Jim McClaren did a lot of work for the Nature Conservancy place further up the coast. Roddy's a practical lad, too. Have you seen inside that workshop of his.

Neil nodded. 'He's mending our boat in there at the moment.'

The man looked at him thoughtfully. 'A sailing

dinghy with red sails?'

'That's it.'

'Dear me, then I believe I owe you an apology. I nearly collided with you in the mouth of the harbour the other day. Downing's the name. I'm a guest of Colonel Murdoch at the big house. You did a swift bit of avoiding action, lad. Well done!'

Neil looked pleased, but Lynette still felt awkward.

Mr Downing moved his walking stick from one hand to the other. 'I feel I owe you an explanation as well as an apology. Colonel Murdoch had my car for the day and lent me his boat in exchange. I was having a look round the area when a movement on the hill caught my eye, hence my lack of concentration. No damage done, I hope?'

'Not then,' said Neil. 'There was this morning, though, by someone else. And now there's a dirty great hole in the side.'

'They came from nowhere and made us hit a rock,' Lynette said.

Mr Downing frowned. 'Deliberately? Are you sure?'

'It wasn't Rowena's fault. There was no time to do anything.'

'And where was this?'

'Near Coronsay, the island over there.'

'What did your parents have to say about that?'

Neil made a face. 'They'd be furious and blame Rowena if they knew. They've gone to Nabble Pin . . . you know, the high peak to the north of Butallie. Roddy's in charge of us. He's doing the boat now.'

'So it's likely to be out of action for a few days?'

'The primer has to dry,' said Neil. 'And at least two coats of paint.'

Mr Downing nodded as if satisfied about something. 'I see. Well, good luck with your sailing in the future. And keep well away from trouble.'

'We will,' they chorused. But as soon as he had gone

they smiled at each other, and Neil said what was in Lynette's thoughts. 'Good thing Toby didn't hear that. Toby likes trouble, doesn't he?'

'You'll tell your dad, though, won't you?'

Neil shrugged. 'The hole will be mended by then. It won't look so bad, and I don't suppose he'll mind much.'

Later, back at the cottage and almost ready for bed, Lynette made up her mind to say something about the accident. A small peat fire smouldered on the grate, and Aunt Ruth had just made mugs of cocoa for all of them.

'I sailed with Rowena today,' she said, with both hands round her mug for warmth. 'There was a bit of trouble. We holed the boat, and Roddy's mending it.'

'It's all right,' Toby said quickly. 'They hit a rock, but it's all right.'

Uncle Alec took a long drink and placed his mug on a table at his side. 'So that's what you were all doing in Butallie. In Roddy's workshop, eh? Made a fine job of it did he?'

'Roddy's great,' Toby said enthusiastically. 'When he's finished working on it no one will ever know there was ever a gash in the side. I wish I was as clever as that.'

'I thought the lassie was a good sailor. Your fault then was it, Lynette?'

She looked at him quickly and saw that his eyes were twinkling. 'We nearly collided with someone in a motor boat. They were there so suddenly.'

Toby looked indignant. 'They did it on purpose. Steam gives way to sail. Everyone knows that.'

'Not people unused to boats,' said Uncle Alec.

Aunt Ruth looked concerned. 'Most holiday people are away home now.'

'Aye, that's so. They'll likely have been as concerned

as you, and it'll not happen again. You're not worried, lass?'

Lynette hesitated. 'Not worried exactly. But two people came to Coronsay yesterday. They didn't stay long, but we couldn't see what they were doing.'

Aunt Ruth reached for her cocoa, and took a sip. 'And why was that?'

'We were hiding.'

Uncle Alec laughed. 'Smugglers is it then, Toby? Or was it pirates you were suspecting?'

'Lynette thinks they were digging up flowers,' Tony said hotly. 'She's going to take her flower book over there to find out which ones they're taking.'

'But who were they?' their aunt asked. 'Not local people?'

Lynette shook her head. 'I don't think so. A man and a woman.'

'You won't be a nuisance to anyone, will you?'

'Leave them be, Ruth. They've got sense.' Uncle Alec grinned at Toby. 'So you want a trip over there tomorrow?'

'Can you maroon us again, Uncle Alec? Neil, too. Roddy'll be busy on *Seaspray*. Can we go round to Butallie and pick Neil up?'

'If you promise not to trap any brigands, or those pirates of yours.'

'You will be careful, won't you?' Aunt Ruth said anxiously. 'Make sure you don't cause any trouble. But Mr and Mrs Havill will have other plans for their family, maybe.'

But they hadn't. It was arranged that the Craigs and Havills would be picked up from Coronsay again after lunch and brought back to Butallie to spend the rest of the day there with Roddy.

As they set off for the island through the smooth water Lynette wondered what force had been used to get Rowena to go with them when she would plainly much rather have stayed behind. Rowena, as usual, was silent. Her face looked pale, and there were dark shadows beneath her eyes.

'Is your ankle hurting?' Lynette asked her.

Rowena shrugged. 'Not much.'

Lynette thought about the sailing they had done together yesterday, and the way Rowena had hitched her feet beneath the toe strap when she had leaned out. It must have hurt her, whatever she said.

'I've brought my flower book,' she said. 'I thought you might like to look in it for a little mauve flower. I've got a feeling those people were looking for it, and I don't know what it is.'

Rowena made no answer. Lynette gave up and glanced at the two boys sitting together in the bows with their heads close together. Neil's camera was hanging round his neck on its long strap. She guessed they were talking about the intruders and making plans.

As soon as they had waded ashore and waved goodbye to their uncle, Lynette took their rucksack and Neil and Rowena's bag to Shanvara. Neil had his camera stuffed in his pocket by now so that it wouldn't get in the way when he was bending down.

By the time she had made sure that no one else had been there the boys were on the low headland, busy searching. Then all three of them spread out over the hillside, the boys racing ahead to get to the top of Ben Vara first. They stood against the skyline, side by side, Neil tall and slim with his mass of hair yellow in the sunshine and Toby small and wiry beside him.

'You can be seen from miles around,' she shouted up to them.

At once they threw themselves to the ground and wriggled down towards her.

'It's no good,' Toby gasped as they came close. 'We haven't found *anything*.'

Neil sat up, and rubbed his face. 'What's Rowena doing?'

They all looked down at the headland that looked flat and small from above. Rowena was kneeling to look at something on the ground.

'She's found that flower of yours,' Toby shouted, leaping up. They ran down the hill to join her.

'Is this it?' she asked, sitting back on her heels.

Lynette smiled. 'Where did you find it?' She took the flower from her very gently. It lay in her hand, its four mauve petals looking translucent in the sunshine.

Rowena smiled too, and her dark eyes lit up. 'Where's your book? Aren't you going to identify it?'

Lynette ran to Shanvara to get it, and then back again.

'There are hundreds of flowers in here,' Toby said in disgust as he watched her turn the pages.

'It's got four petals,' she said. 'That's unusual. Most have got five. Is there a leaf, Rowena?'

Rowena nodded, and handed one to her. Lynette touched it gently with one finger, and then looked in her book again. 'I don't think we're going to find it in here. It must be very rare.'

'Rare enough for the Rammers to want it,' said Toby triumphantly.

Neil took his camera out of its case. 'You don't really think that, do you? Hold it still. I'll take two photos, just in case.'

Lynette closed the book. 'Thanks Neil. Those people seemed to be after something.'

Rowena tossed her head. 'They were desperate enough to want *us* out of the way, anyway.'

This was the first time she had wanted to join in with them, and Lynette was pleased. She walked by Rowena's side when they went to Shanvara to get their food to eat on the beach. Afterwards Rowena helped pack the bags again ready for the return of Uncle Alec's motor boat.

When it was done the boys ran off up the hill again searching for more of the flowers.'

'I wish we didn't have to go so soon,' Lynette said. 'I really like it here. At first, I wasn't so sure . . . that is, when we had seen you sailing past and it got dark and you didn't come back.'

To her dismay Rowena blushed a fiery red. 'Why should you worry? It wasn't your problem. You like interfering in other people's lives. Like today. Who said I wanted to come here? No one, but they made me just because of Neil.'

'We had to find out what the Rammers were looking for,' said Lynette.

'More sense to go scouting round in Roddy's boat instead. We might have seen them, and got a better idea what they were up to.'

'I'm surprised Neil didn't want to,' said Lynette. 'But you two aren't much alike are you?'

Rowena glared at Lynette. 'It's all right for you,' she burst out passionately. 'It doesn't matter if you're not like Toby. You don't know what it's like not to belong, to be the odd one out. *You* weren't adopted. I only found *that* out just before we came on holiday. They were too scared to tell me before.'

Surprised, Lynette stared back at her. Rowena's words seemed to hang ominously on the air, and she didn't know what to say. She watched Rowena stumble to her feet and go off across the beach to sit down on a rock at the other side with her back to her.

She knew it was important to reach Rowena. 'Please God,' she prayed. 'Please help me to help her. Please tell me what to say.'

She remained for a few moments with her head bent and her eyes closed, concentrating on Rowena. Never for one moment had she guessed what troubled her. How could she? She seemed like an ordinary member of the Havill family, and really she was.

It took a great deal of courage to get up at last and walk down across the sand to Rowena and sit down at her side. 'It was great, finding that mauve flower. I've put it in a safe place. Thanks, Rowena.'

'I don't see what good it's going to do if we can't find out what it's called,' Rowena muttered.

Lynette was silent. When she was with the boys she was as excited about the find as they were, but now, sitting here on the rocks with Rowna, she began to see it through her eyes. Her own good sense, too, told her that Toby liked to pretend. Suppose it was just a game they were playing, and not serious at all?

'But you agree they're after something?' she said diffidently.

'You were in *Seaspray* weren't you?' Rowena said. 'That was deliberate, if anything was. It's no game they're playing.'

Lynette looked at her in surprise. 'How did you know what I was thinking?'

'Anyone can tell.'

'So they really were trying to frighten us away from the island?'

Rowena shrugged. 'Of course they were. Wasn't it obvious? Flower or not, they're doing something they shouldn't. And *I* mean to find out what it is whether the rest of you like it or not.'

Chapter Seven

Rowena stood tensely at the water's edge, shading her eyes and muttering that they should have been collected from Coronsay by now. Lynette had placed the mauve flower and its leaf carefully inside the lunch box which she held in her hand instead of putting it sideways into the rucksack.

They were all relieved when at last they saw Uncle Alec's boat coming round the headland.

'What have you got there?' Uncle Alec asked Lynette as they climbed aboard.

'A flower we found,' Lynette said. 'It's not in my book.'

'So *that's* the buried treasure?'

'It wasn't buried,' Toby called back from the bows where he was sitting with Neil. 'We told you, Uncle. Those people were digging them up all over the place. That's the only one we found.'

'Then maybe you should have left it there.'

'We've got it for identifying,' Lynette said. 'We only picked the flower. At home it's illegal to dig up the roots. I expect it's the same here.'

'Aye. Well, I can't help you with that. Maybe Roddy can, or his mother.'

Lynette smiled. 'We're going to show it to him as soon as we get back.'

All this time Rowena had been sitting silently with her back to them. Now she glanced round impatiently as they passed the harbour entrance on their way to Butallie. She stood up as they approached the jetty, balancing on one foot and leaning on the gunwale.

Inside his workshop Roddy was still busy. The side of the boat where the hole had been was now rubbed down smoothly, and if it hadn't been for the different colour they would hardly have seen where the piece of wood had been inserted.

'That's great,' said Neil.

Roddy had dust on his bare head, and there were shadows of fatigue round his eyes.

Toby gazed admiringly at *Seaspray*. 'Have you much more to do? Do you need some help?'

'There's cleaning up to be done, right enough,' Roddy said. 'Then I'll do the top coat.'

Nimrod, the black cat, appeared out of the shadows and wound himself round Rowena's ankles. At once she stooped to pick him up, crooning softly to him. She seemed completely different from the dark brooding Rowena that Lynette was used to. Even her face looked softer.

'I'd better do the finding out about the mauve flower myself,' Lynette said. 'I'll go and ask Roddy's mother.'

Neil went with her. Mrs McClaren was in the shop, dusting some shelves. She stopped what she was doing at once, and turned to them, smiling. 'Now, what can I do for you, my dears?'

Lynette had brought the lunch box with her. She opened it, and lifted out the small flower. 'We wondered if you might know what this is?'

Mrs McClaren peered at it, and shook her head. 'I've never seen one like it, to my knowledge. Where did you find it?'

'Over on the island.' Lynette replaced it in the box, looking crestfallen. 'We thought you might know.'

'The gentleman staying with Colonel Murdoch might,' Mrs McClaren said doubtfully. 'I expect you've seen him about? He comes in here sometimes. He used to know my husband.'

Lynette brightened. 'Mr Downing? Do you think he would?'

'He's a clever man. He doesn't work much now, I believe, but he used to help solve crimes. Roddy's father always . . .'

Neil's eyes widened. 'Solved crimes? You mean, he's a policeman?'

Mrs McClaren shook her head. 'Not a policeman, no. You were saying about the flower?'

Neil looked as if he was bursting to ask more about Mr Downing's work, but Mrs McClaren pressed her lips together and seemed not to want to say any more.

They met Mr Downing on the way to the colonel's house. He moved his walking stick from one hand to the other as Lynette told him about Rowena finding the plant and how they needed to identify it.

He took the box from her, and looked at the plant, frowning. 'Where did you find this?'

'There aren't many of them . . .' Lynette began.

Neil chipped in quickly, 'Some people came to the island. Lynette thinks they're stealing these flowers. They're looking for earth samples, *I* think.'

Mr Downing cocked an eyebrow at him. 'So you don't go much on flowers?'

Neil grinned. 'What can you do with a flower except put it in water, and smell it?'

Mr Downing smiled at him, and then listened to what Lynette had to say with a serious expression on his face. She had expected a few joking remarks like Uncle Alec's, so was surprised.

'Toby found a penknife the other day,' she said. 'I'd forgotten about it till now.' She felt in her pocket, and pulled the penknife out to show him. 'That's what made us think . . . it *must* have been theirs, the two people we saw.'

54

'May I see?' Mr Downing handed back the lunch box and took the penknife from her instead. 'Do you mind if I keep this for the time being?'

Lynette shook her head She could think only of the flower. 'And you don't know what it is?'

Mr Downing smiled. 'My host, Colonel Murdoch, has a fine library in his house. I'm sure he'd be only too pleased to put it at your disposal.

'He'd let us look it up in one of his books? We'd be very careful, wouldn't we Neil?'

'There's no time like the present. Come with me, both of you.'

'But why do you want the penknife?' Neil asked.

'I'm afraid I can't say at the moment. I'll see you get it back, I promise. Will that do?'

'Are you a detective?'

Mr Downing's eyes crinkled at the corners as he smiled and shook his head. 'Let's say I have a particular interest in this area at the moment. You do promise me to keep well away from any trouble, don't you? I shall have a word with Roddy.'

Colonel Murdoch's house was set back from the road among a group of trees. The large front door stood open. Their footsteps made no sound as they followed Mr Downing up to the first floor landing and into a room on the right. Most of the wall space from floor to ceiling was covered with bookcases.

Neil stared at them open-mouthed. 'Wow!'

Mr Downing went to the shelves opposite the door. He placed his stick against the shelves, and then moved a short pair of steps to where he wanted them.

'There are several volumes about wild flowers here,' he said as he climbed stiffly up the steps to reach down three large brown books.

The mauve flower and its spiky leaf were looking decidedly crumpled by this time. Mr Downing had another close look at them before handing them back to Lynette.

They set to work. Lynette's cheeks were flushed with excitement as she leafed through the book in front of her.

The telephone rang in the distance, and Mr Downing got to his feet. 'Take as long as you like,' he said as he walked to the door.

Lynette's book *A Naturalist in the North* by James McCulloch, looked more promising than Neil's because the illustrations were in colour.

'This is it!' she cried after a few minutes. 'Look, Neil, the leaves are the same, and the flower has four petals. I'm sure it's the one.'

He came and stood behind her.

'Coronwort.' Lynette's voice was shaky with excitement. 'The Latin name is *glaux foemina*. There's another one called *glaux maritima*. That's more common. I've got that in my little flower book.' She ran her finger down the page of print under *glaux foemina*. 'It's a rare plant, and almost extinct.'

'You mean, it's *really* rare?'

'Almost extinct, it says. We've found what those people are after. It *must* be, Neil!' She looked up with shining eyes.

'But what would they want it for? It's crazy.'

'It's too much of a coincidence for a rare plant to be growing on Coronsay when we suspect them of digging something up. Have you got it in your book?'

Neil sat down again, and turned to the index. 'It gives two page numbers.' He turned to the first and Lynette leaned across to look. There was a small black and white illustration which they wouldn't have recognised if they hadn't known what it was. Neil waded through the second page of print as quickly as he could.

'There's no more here than in yours,' he said at last. 'A rare plant, found only in the north of the country, and then they give a long description of it.' He shut the book. 'Coronwort, and we found it on Coronsay. The island is called after the flower. It must be very import-ant, and we've found it!'

'Or the flower was named after the island.' Lynette pulled the book towards her as Neil got up and climbed up the steps. She wanted to read as much about it as she could for herself.

'There are all sorts of books here,' Neil said. 'No more flower books, though, or we might have found out some more.' He leapt off, moved the steps further along, and jumped up on them again. 'Just imagine having all these books. He must like reading.'

'Or finding things out,' Lynette said, deep in the flower book.

'He must know an awful lot.' Neil was amusing him-self leaping up and down, and looking in some of the books which he replaced carefully.

'Here are some on religion, millions of them.'

Lynette looked up. 'What sort of religion?'

Neil climbed down. 'See for yourself.'

It felt strange being up so high. She looked down on the room, at the large polished table and the three books Mr Downing had selected for them that lay open. Looking back at the shelves she saw that some of the books were Bibles, and there were several hymn books too, and some large volumes of Bible commentaries like her father had in his study at home. Home? She shivered. It wasn't going to be home for much longer.

'What's it like having a vicar for a dad?' Neil called up to her. 'I bet he hasn't got as many books as these.'

Lynette selected a small book from the shelf in front of her, and opened it. She saw that it was a book of daily readings from the Bible and covered a different subject each week. At the end it gave the references to the Bible.

Thoughtfully she brought it down to the table to look

at more closely. 'Why should he be any different from any other dad?' she asked as she sat down to read.

'Well he only works on Sundays for a start.'

She was used to this one. 'He works *every* day.' Her eye was caught by the theme for the week before last . . . Family. It seemed to have lots to say about this, and she had just started to read when Neil came back to join her.

'What have you found?' he asked.

'I wish I could borrow it,' she said. 'I want to read what it says here about families. It's important.'

'Families? Don't talk to me about families. You should have a sister like Rowena!'

Lynette put her finger in the book as she looked up. 'Well . . . we were talking this morning and she told me she didn't know she was adopted and . . .'

'She *told* you?' Neil looked amazed. 'Now *that* I can hardly believe. It's her secret, and I'm never allowed to say. That's why she's spoilt. Mum lets her do anything she likes, but if I want to do anything, well . . .'

'She didn't want to come to Coronsay with us this morning.'

'Only because we couldn't sail. And she doesn't like your uncle.'

Lynette was surprised. 'Uncle Alec? But everyone likes Uncle Alec.'

'Not my sister.'

'Why not?'

Neil shrugged. 'How would I know? *I* like him.'

Lynette looked down at the booklet once more. In her mind she had a picture of Uncle Alec carrying Rowna down to the boat because she had hurt her ankle. She tried to imagine what it would feel like, knowing you'd done something stupid and having to be rescued in front of Toby and herself who were younger. Maybe if she was Rowena she wouldn't like Uncle Alec much for embarrassing her even though it was her own fault.

Neil and her father had been waiting on the jetty for Rowena, each reacting in a different way to what she had done. Family relationships again, she thought.

She reached for one of the pencils in the centre of the table and wrote the Bible references on the note pad nearby. 'Ephesians chapter 3 verse 15,' she murmured as she wrote. 'Ephesians 6:4, 1 Timothy 5:1 to 4, and chapter 6 verse 2, and some more.' Then she hastily tore off the leaf of paper and put it in the box with the coronwort flower. She could look up the verses for herself later and find out what the Bible had to say about families.

'We've found what we came for anyway,' Neil said cheerfully. 'And I think you're right. That's what those Rammers were after!'

Suddenly Lynette had a peculiar feeling. She and Toby had found *three* paper cups left behind on Coronsay that first day. Suppose Mr Downing had something to do with the Rammers? He was in the boat that had nearly collided with *Seaspray* that first day. 'We've been a bit stupid to come here on our own like this,' she muttered. 'We'd better go.'

She left the booklet on the table with the others, and was half-way to the door before Neil got up and followed her. Outside, her fears seemed ludicrous. Mr Downing, elderly and well-dressed, a guest of Colonel Murdoch and once a friend of Roddy's father, couldn't possibly have anything to do with the Rammers. Or could he? Perhaps he was in disguise.

Toby came running towards them. 'Roddy's finished the boat!' he shouted. 'Come and see. It's as good as new. Did you find out the name of the flower?'

As Neil looked up at the sky heavy rain began to fall. They ran as fast as they could to the workshop.

Chapter Eight

They rushed inside. The rain had turned to hail which beat like bullets on the workshop's corrugated roof. *Seaspray*'s white hull shone in the gloom.

'Roddy's done a good job,' Toby cried. 'Come and see.'

Neil shook his head hard and raindrops flew around him. He inspected Roddy's work carefully. 'It's great, Roddy. When can we sail again?'

'Not in this weather. The paint'll need to harden anyway.'

As Roddy started to clean his paintbrush Lynette explained about meeting Mr Downing and finding out that the mauve flower was called coronwort.

'Mr Downing said he used to know your father,' she said.

Roddy finished what he was doing, and looked up. 'Aye.'

'So he can't have anything to do with the Rammers then.' She couldn't help remembering how she had felt in Colonel Murdoch's house. But Roddy knew Mr Downing. That, surely, was proof enough? Even so she couldn't quite stifle the feeling that Mr Downing wasn't what he was pretending to be. Yet he didn't seem a bit like those other two they had seen on the island. Suddenly she smiled.

'What's up?' Toby demanded. He looked at her suspiciously. 'You're laughing!'

Her eyes danced. 'I was trying to imagine Mr Downing wearing jeans.'

Neil looked as if he didn't know whether to laugh or not. 'Jeans . . . why jeans?'

'Suppose he's one of them – one of the Rammers, a sort of secret agent for them. He could be.'

'You mean if he's one of the Rammers he ought to look like them? But no, not that old man with the serious face and the walking stick.'

'I followed you down the road for a bit,' Rowena said suddenly. 'I saw him. His eyes were sharp. I saw them looking.'

'Looking at what?'

'As if he could see things we couldn't.'

Neil ran his hand through his fair hair making it stand up like yellow straw. 'If he *is* a Rammer then he knows things we don't. Taking us up to that library could be part of his plot to make us think the flower's important when it isn't.

'I'm sure it is,' Lynette said quickly, her amusement gone now.

'Of *course* it is.' Rowena sounded quite sure as she supported her weight on the boat.

Neil frowned. 'But the phone call that got him out of the library was convenient, too convenient. D'you think it wasn't for him at all but was an excuse for him to warn the others that we know what they're up to?'

'But we don't, not for sure,' said Toby. He kicked his toe in the dust of the workshop impatiently. It was all right for Lynette to talk about the flower, but Neil ought to be helping him plan how they could get the Rammers for damaging *Seaspray*.

'Mr Downing's clever,' Lynette said doubtfully.

'Too clever,' said Neil with feeling.

Rowena moved slightly against the boat as Roddy came back to finish his clearing up. 'And we won't trust Mr Downing one inch. What do you say, Roddy?'

Roddy looked pre-occupied as if he hadn't really heard. He glanced round for the cloth he had been using so he could wipe his hands. 'Aye. We'll not trust anyone.'

For once they were all as one, and Lynette smiled. Rowena seemed aware of an unusual closeness too as the boys finished the clearing up. There was a friendliness that hadn't been there before. Perhaps Rowena had been thinking things out for herself. Dad said that God spoke to people in different ways.

Neil rummaged in the bag for some peppermints and handed them round. 'You should have seen all the books Colonel Murdoch's got. A whole room full of them with a little step ladder to reach the top shelves.

'What sort of books?' asked Toby glumly.

All sorts. Three huge flower books. That's how we found out about coronwort being very rare. Books on religion . . .'

Rowena was startled. 'Religion?'

Neil laughed. 'Lynette copied something down from one of them.'

'It's something I want to look up in my Bible. About families.'

'What about families?' Rowena asked suspiciously. She didn't wait for an answer but went to the open doorway and looked out at the sodden world. The hail had given way to rain now, and low cloud veiled the hills.

Toby swallowed his peppermint and took another from the packet Neil held out to him. 'But what about the flower? What else did it *say* about it?'

Lynette was glad to get back to the flower books. 'It gave the Latin name, *glaux foemina*. I think that's pretty. It grows in the north of the country like another one of the same family, *glaux maritima*, but ours is almost extinct now. That's why I think those people were looking for it.'

'And we found it,' Toby said with satisfaction.

Lynette smiled. 'I'm sure that's what they were digging up. All those little holes . . .'

'But what *for*?' Neil said. 'I mean, what will they do with them? I think you're right though . . . since we've found it's rare you must be. I still want to know *why*.'

'Don't we all?' said Rowena from the doorway.

Roddy looked across at her broodingly. 'Aye, if you're right, Lynette, they were stealing right enough. Coronwort on Coronsay. That flower will have bloomed over there on the island for centuries. No one has the right to dig it up and take it away.'

'But we can't stop them,' said Neil.

Rowena spun round. 'Oh can't we?'

Roddy didn't answer, but pulled his bush hat more firmly on his head. There was a gleam in his eyes that promised no good for anyone who tried to steal anything from a place he loved.

'So what are we going to do?' Toby asked hopefully.

'We'll spy on them,' Rowena said as she came away from the doorway and sat down on a pile of boxes. 'We'll make plans.' Her dark eyes sparkled. 'We'd better get back to the island as soon as we can and be ready for them.'

Toby looked as if he was gong to burst with excitement. 'We can jump out at them and frighten them.'

Lynette sat down too. 'But Toby, Uncle Alec wouldn't approve of that.'

'He won't be there,' Rowena retorted.

There was silence for a moment, and they could still hear the rain drumming on the tin roof. Even if *Seaspray* wasn't out of action they couldn't do anything else today. Lynette began to wish they were back at the cottage waiting for the high tea Aunt Ruth would have ready for them.

But Rowena, her cheeks glowing, was full of how

they were going to catch the Rammers, and Toby was chipping in with what they would do to them when they caught them. It was fast turning into make-believe, one of Toby's pretending games.

Lynette glanced at Roddy and saw the thoughtful expression on his face. He removed his hat and scratched his head. Was he taking it as seriously as she was herself?

He felt her looking at him, and turned and smiled. 'We'll go back to the island tomorrow in *Shona*, maybe. No harm in that. Plenty of mackerel to catch for lunch. We'll cook it over there.'

At once his words made things seem ordinary again. That was what she and Toby had done on their first morning. She suddenly smelt the imaginary smell of sizzling mackerel, and felt hungry. Then she thought of the mackerel Roddy's mother had cooked for them yesterday when they had been miserable about the damage to *Seaspray*.

They had crowded into Mrs McClaren's small room behind the shop yesterday, leaving Roddy engrossed in what he was doing.

'Aye, he'll be in soon enough,' his mother had said in her warm voice as she placed a dish of oatmeal-covered mackerel in front of them. There were plates of thick buttered bread, too, and a large pot of tea.

Soon the four of them were eating as if they hadn't had a meal for weeks. Roddy's mother looked on approvingly, holding Nimrod tightly in her arms. He was looking more than interested and was uttering little mews as they ate. Once the shop bell rang and she disappeared for a few minutes, still holding Nimrod.

On the walls were pictures of animals in thick dark frames, deer and wildcats and red squirrels. There was a shelf of books, too, and Lynette saw two old Bibles side by side, with dim gold lettering on their spines.

When Mrs McClaren returned she had Mr and Mrs Havill with her, and Roddy came in soon afterwards. The room that had seemed crowded before was jam-packed now.

'We caught the fish ourselves,' said Neil. 'That's why they tasted so good.'

Rowena was now holding Nimrod, and feeding him with scraps from her own plate.

Mrs McClaren laughed as she saw it. 'He's got a friend, that one,' she said.

'And so have we in Roddy,' said Mr Havill. 'Your son's dealt admirably with the damage to the boat. I've been discussing it all with him, and we've come to an arrangement.'

To the relief of all of them he had made no trouble about the sailing, and had brushed off Neil's remarks about none of it being Rowena's fault with a wave of his hand. It was Rowena's mother who seemed as if she was going to make difficulties.

'Your foot, Rowena,' she said anxiously. 'Are you sure you're not overdoing it? I really think . . .'

'What d'you think? That I can't cope?'

Mrs Havill flushed. 'Now don't start that . . .'

Rowena got up, and stood glowering. 'It's always the same. The minute I want to do something . . .'

'I let you do it,' her mother said quickly. 'That's obviously where I've gone wrong in the past. I'm not sure that . . .'

Her father laughed easily. 'She'll be all right. We know our Rowena!'

Mrs Havill shrugged, but she was smiling now. Only Rowena still scowled.

So now it was only the weather that would stop them. The rain was a thin drizzle, but the visibility was bad. Toby went to the door of the workshop and looked out hopefully.

'It won't be any good at the moment,' Neil said, behind him. 'You heard what Roddy said about the paint hardening.'

'We'd better get back to the cottage,' Lynette said. 'So what plans do we have for tomorrow?'

'Coronsay, of course,' Rowena said. 'We'll meet there very early.'

'The top of Ben Vara makes a good look-out,' said Toby enthusiastically.

After tea Lynette brought her Bible downstairs. She sat at the table close to the fire. The peat glowed in the hearth and the dry scent of it filled the small room at the front of the cottage and made her forget the dreary greyness outside. She couldn't even see the harbour when she glanced out of the window. It was an evening for the fireside and no mistake, as Uncle Alec said.

He was seated opposite her at the table with the newspaper while her aunt was clattering things about in the kitchen. Toby, on the hearthrug, was deep in his sailing book.

'What are you doing, lass?' Uncle Alec asked.

She looked up, with her finger against the Bible references she had jotted down on the piece of paper in Colonel Murdoch's library.

'I'm looking up about family relationships,' she said.

Uncle Alec looked startled, and his paper rustled. 'Nothing wrong with yours, surely? You're not still worried about the move, are you, lassie? Your father was saying it's going to be hard for you.'

Now it was her turn to look surprised. 'Did Dad really say that? I talked to Mum about it and I suppose she told Dad I didn't want to move.'

He laughed. 'Are you reading that bit about fathers not goading their children but bringing them up in the nurture and admonition of the Lord? That comes in Paul's letter to the Ephesians, doesn't it?'

'It's different in mine.' Lynette read from the Bible. ' "Parents, do not treat your children in such a way as to make them angry. Instead bring them up with Christian discipline and instruction." '

His eyes twinkled in his tanned face. 'But surely your father has given you loving instruction. And he hasn't angered you, has he? Or is it this move to Dankford that angers you?'

'Of course it doesn't,' she said indignantly. 'I know Dad feels it's the right thing to do, that he's needed in Dankford. I thought he knew that. So how does he know I'm a bit worried?'

He smiled. 'He loves you, lassie, that's how.'

Lynette gazed thoughtfully at the Bible in front of her. 'I'll get used to the move. I've prayed hard. I know it will be all right.' But her lips trembled a little as she felt Uncle Alec's concern for her.

She concentrated hard on the words on the open page, reading a few verses before the one she had looked up first. 'Listen Uncle, "Children, it is your Christian duty to obey your parents, for this is the right thing to do. Respect your father and mother is the first commandment that has a promise added: So that all may go well with you, and you may live a long time in the land." ' She looked up. 'That's better. But I don't really understand what it means. How *can* doing that make you live long in the land?'

'It needs thinking about,' Uncle Alec said. Then he put his paper down again, looking suddenly serious. 'Lassie if there really *is* something wrong you'd better tell me.'

'Not with me,' she said hurriedly. 'It's something different. It's Rowena, you see.'

'Still up to her tricks, is she?' He looked at her closely. 'It was like she said, wasn't it, when we found her and her boat in the inlet? She had landed to explore and fell and injured her ankle. She wasn't playing up and doing it deliberately?'

'No, oh no!' Lynette was horrified. 'Nothing like that, honestly. It's just that she's got a problem and I want to help her. She minds desperately about something, and I was looking in the Bible to see what it says about family relationships.'

Uncle Alec disappeared behind his paper again. 'Then I won't pry. Just let me know if you need help with anything.'

There was silence for a few minutes while Lynette rustled the pages of her Bible. At last she said, 'Uncle Alec, it's no good. The bits I've looked up are all about parents being good to their children. That's not what I really want. I'll have to go on looking.'

'Remember, though, lassie, that you're on sticky ground with that one. Quoting Bible verses at her isn't going to make much difference to her in the mood she's been in every time I've seen her.'

Lynette sighed, and closed her Bible. Dad had often said that you must wait for people to ask for help when they're ready. Somehow she thought that with the search for the Rammers and revenge uppermost in Rowena's mind, that moment wasn't going to come.

Chapter Nine

Toby let out a sudden yell as they approached Coronsay's silver beach in *Shona* next day. The others stared round at him in amazement.

'What did you do that for?' Neil asked indignantly when he had recovered.

Lynette looked at him expectantly. 'Did you see them, Toby?'

He shook his head, and pursed his lips to let rip again, but Rowena sprang forward and held her hand over his mouth.

'Stop that!' Roddy ordered. He glared at Rowena as she let go immediately and Toby, rubbing his mouth, retired muttering to the bows.

Every now and again Roddy looked anxiously out to sea where an ominous bank of cloud hung over the horizon.

'Seagull signals,' Toby called back to the others. 'That's what it sounded like, didn't it? A seagull calling out at sea.'

'More like a banshee,' Rowena said bitterly. 'Tell me next time you want to do it and I'll jump overboard.'

Lynette giggled, and Neil shrugged his shoulders. He leaned over the side as far as he could without falling out.

'It's hard to judge the depth,' he said. 'It looks shallow, but I know it isn't. Look at all that hard sand down there.'

But Toby, intent on his good idea, took no notice of him. 'It's because we're too close to each other,' he said instead. 'If we were further apart, say one on the island and the rest here, it would sound real.'

'It was more like a foghorn,' Roddy said.

Toby grinned, but said no more for the moment as they neared the beach and the anchor was thrown overboard. For a while there was the business of getting themselves and all their gear to dry land without dropping anything.

But when it had all been stowed away in Shanvara, except for Neil's camera, and Roddy had been shown how he and Lynette had made the hide-out against the hollow in the cliffs, Toby raised the question of seagull signals again.

'We ought to be able to communicate with each other in secret if any of us find the Rammers,' he said. 'Don't you think it's a good idea? One call repeated over and over again could mean *attention*.'

Rowena's eyes shone. 'I see what you mean. Well done, Toby! Someone's got some sense. 'Two calls for *message received*.'

'Wait,' said Lynette. 'We must write these down. Just a minute while I get a paper and pencil.'

Luckily she had brought some in the rucksack. She was back from Shanvara almost at once and kneeling in the sand ready to act as scribe.

'Seagull Signals,' she wrote.

'One call, repeated: *attention*!
Two calls: *message received*.
Three calls: *please repeat message*.
Four calls: *danger*!
Five calls: *on guard, something about to happen*.
Six calls: *come here at once*.'

She stopped writing, and looked at them doubtfully.

'It'll do for now,' said Rowena. 'We'll learn these first. And we'll have to practise.'

Toby leapt up. 'I'll go up to the top of Ben Vara. I can do a bit of spying at the same time.'

'We'll wait,' said Roddy. 'We'll plan this properly. Time enough later for spying. We'll stay here and learn the signals first, right enough. Inside Shanvara, everyone.'

'But what happens if the Rammers come and we don't see them?' Toby objected.

'And what are we going to do about it if we do?' said Lynette as she got to her feet.

But Roddy was firm. 'First things first. We need to be able to communicate with each other. The idea is to make quite sure of what they're up to. We need proof, but that's not so easy. Being able to signal to each other is important.'

It didn't take them very long after all. Rowena learnt the signals almost at once. She went to the doorway and peered outside. 'No one there. Now's the time to go and practise.'

'Off you go, Neil and Toby,' Roddy said. 'And Toby, make sure it sounds like real seagulls. Don't forget to keep your heads down.'

They were off at once, wriggling up the hill through the heather, while the others spread themselves over the island, hiding as well as they could in case any strangers were about.

Toby was the first to signal with one call, then a pause, and another, and a pause. There were answering double calls from different directions, some weaker than others as if the human seagulls making them were not quite sure of the sounds that filled the quiet air.

'They heard!' Neil said in suppressed excitement. 'My turn now.'

But before he could get enough breath in his lungs someone else was having a go.

'*Attention* again,' said Toby. 'That's no good.'

Beside him Neil signalled that he'd understood the

message.

Toby covered his ears. 'You'd hear that on the mainland,' he said.

Neil laughed, and tried again, this time signalling *something about to happen*. 'I wish it really was,' he said as he crouched down beside Toby to wait for the others to signal *message received*.

When at last they had all had the chance to signal and make a reply, and the real Coronsay seagulls had got over their shock, Roddy gave the signal from Shanvara.

'Six calls,' said Toby. '*Come here at once*. We've got to go back.'

They were the last there. The others were talking about other ways of signalling if they were in sight of each other but out of earshot.

'But we won't be out of earshot on Coronsay,' said Toby.

'Who says we'll *be* on Coronsay?' Rowena demanded. 'We could be anywhere once *Seaspray*'s ready.'

Lynette looked at her doubtfully, and was glad when Neil raised the subject of food.

'Aye,' said Roddy. 'No harm in that. Anyone see anything suspicious?'

They shook their heads. There hadn't been sight of anyone.

'Let's eat on the hill to keep a look-out at the same time,' said Rowena.

It seemed a good plan, and they all helped to carry the lunch things to the top of Ben Vara, and then spread themselves out a little so someone could see in every direction.

'Not a bad view if you're into scenery,' Rowena said as she sat down in the heather with her legs stretched out in front of her. 'So what will we do if we're out of earshot?'

'Morse code,' said Roddy. 'But that takes too long to

learn, right enough. And we've no equipment.'

Lynette got out the container of ham-filled baps from her rucksack and handed them round. 'I started learning it at Guides once. E I S H are the dots. E one dot, I two dots, S three dots and H four dots. And T M and O are the dashes. That bit's easy, but I can't remember any more.'

'Where's the pencil and paper?' asked Neil. He took them from her and began writing it down. 'You can't get much of a message with only seven letters.'

'Tom hit his toe,' said Rowena suddenly.

Lynette laughed. 'Clever!'

'She shot them,' said Roddy.

'If only we could,' said Lynette, her eyes sparkling.

Toby looked from one to the other. 'What are you talking about?'

'The Rammers, of course!'

Roddy looked grim. 'If they're stealing from Coronsay shooting's too good for them.'

Lynette knew he was only half-joking. He wasn't smiling, like the others, and he had eaten hardly anything. He cared about what these people were suspected of doing. He cared badly. Even Rowena was looking happier today, thinking out phrases that used the seven letters, and laughing at some more that Neil came up with.

In the end it was decided that this form of signalling wasn't for them.

'It would take ages to learn, and we haven't the time,' Neil said as he bit into an apple.

For a moment Rowena looked disappointed, but she raised no objection. Lynette was glad it was unanimous. The more things they all agreed about the better.

She hadn't been able to talk to Rowena on her own yet today, and it didn't look as if she would get the opportunity now. And what would she say if she did? She had hoped that the Bible verses she had jotted down might be helpful, but somehow they didn't seem to fit Rowena's situation very well.

Neil gazed around at the empty land and sea. The cloud was disappearing now, and over on the far horizon the sky was the palest blue. 'You're lucky to live near here all the time, Roddy,' he said. 'What does your dad do?'

'Roddy hasn't got a father,' Rowena said. She was sitting with her knees drawn up and her chin on her knees.

'He was a fisherman,' said Roddy. 'Did odd jobs, too, when he could get them. It's three years now since the accident at sea.'

They were all silent for a moment, thinking about it. Toby opened his mouth to ask why Roddy went out fishing so much if that's how his father died, and then shut it again without saying anything.

Lynette was aware that Toby had very nearly said something that was better left unsaid. He looked at her defiantly, and then pulled at another piece of grass to suck.

They had all finished eating now and Toby passed his empty cup across to Lynette.

'Right then,' said Roddy, getting up and pulling his khaki hat down firmly as if the wind was strong enough to blow it off. 'The plans for the afternoon?'

'More practice with signalling,' said Neil.

'Looking to see if we can find any more coronworts,' said Lynette.

'Spying for the Rammers,' said Toby.

'Going searching for them,' said Rowena.

Roddy grinned. 'Right enough. We'll do all of that, if we've time. We'll need to split up. You come with me in *Shona*, Rowena. We'll cruise round about, keeping our eyes skinned.'

'Great!' said Rowena, jumping up.

Neil stuffed some empty containers and Coke tins in

the bag they had brought. 'I'll practise stalking through the heather. And I'll signal every now and again to show where I am because you won't be able to see me.'

'Toby, position yourself somewhere with a good view all round,' Roddy said. 'Here's best.'

Toby looked disappointed. 'Can't I do some stalking too? It's not fair.'

Roddy looked at him sternly. 'It's an important job. None of us will be able to see everything at the same time, only you. Suppose they come and we don't know about it?'

Toby squared his shoulders, already looking for a good place in the heather to hide.

It took some time for everyone to get organised, and even more time for it all to be done. From his hiding place Toby saw Roddy and Rowena paddle out to *Shona*. Seconds later the engine sprang to life, and they were away. At first they were hidden by the hillside but then he could see them again circumnavigating Coronsay, moving very slowly so that anyone watching would think they were out for an afternoon's cruise, and not in search of anything or anyone at all.

Lynette, starting on the low headland, worked methodically, moving backwards and forwards with her head bent low to the ground. Toby knew she would signal the minute she found anything.

He wondered where Neil was, and then saw the heather move half-way down the hill. He tensed as a light flashed, but then realised that it was sunlight reflecting off the lens of Neil's camera. Had he found anything? But no, he was merely messing about with photographs, wasting time.

A second later he tensed again at hearing seagull cries which didn't come from there. For a moment he was startled until he realised that they weren't signals at all, but the real thing. Then, when several came at once from the right place he knew it was Neil, and let out two calls in reply.

The afternoon wore on. On the hilltop Toby began to feel sleepy. It was very boring. The excitement of spying for the Rammers was all very well if they were likely to appear at any moment. But he was beginning to feel now that they never would.

Chapter Ten

When at last Toby saw a boat coming out of the harbour he could hardly believe it. He watched open-mouthed for a few seconds to make quite sure. Yes, it was a small motorboat, and it was heading out to sea. It was the Rammers . . . it must be!

He took a deep breath and let out the loudest signals he had ever made – four calls, *something about to happen*. Then he did it again to make sure. Roddy had heard! The others had, too, because double seagull calls came from different directions.

What luck that *Shona* was cruising on the side of the island hidden from the motor boat. Lynette was on that side, too, on the low headland near the beach.

Toby signalled again. Short single calls, repeated. *Attention! Attention!* He stayed where he was, waiting as patiently as he could for the others to come to him because he couldn't risk losing sight of the boat. It was still going straight out from shore towards the Mellon Isles, not coming towards Coronsay at all.

Neil was the first to come, breathless and excited and wanting to know what Toby had seen. They lay side by side, hardly daring to whisper even though no one in the boat could possibly hear them. Neil was clicking his camera, though, over and over again.

By the time Lynette had reached them the boat was a small speck, and it was almost out of sight by the time Roddy and Rowena arrived.

'There, can you see it?' Neil hissed. 'I've got it on film.'

Roddy's eyes were screwed into tiny slits as if that could make him see better. The boat had gone now, lost among the islands out there across the wide expanse of water.

Rowena sprang up. 'Come on, what are we waiting for? We're wasting time. Let's go and investigate.'

But Roddy didn't move.

'Come *on*, Roddy!'

Neil and Toby stood up, too, now it was safe to do so, but Lynette stayed where she was. She was looking at the Mellon Islands, faintly misty in the grey sea, almost expecting the boat to appear again and ready to signal to the others to get down if it did.

'We stay here,' Roddy said as he got to his feet. 'That was the plan agreed with your father . . . to spend the day on Coronsay, and meet him back at Butallie at six o'clock.'

Rowena's eyes flashed. 'Don't be dismal, Roddy. We'll be back by six easily.'

'There are too many islands, though,' Neil said. 'I wish we had *Seaspray* too, so we could split up.'

'Aye, we'll have the two boats tomorrow right enough.'

Rowena almost spat in her frustration. 'But we've seen them *now*. What good is it tomorrow? I thought you *cared* about Coronsay!'

'Aye, I care.'

'Then *do* something!'

Roddy's voice was like steel. 'We stay here.'

Rowena looked round at the others. 'Come on, you lot. Make him see sense. We'll vote on it.'

But Roddy looked unperturbed. *Shona* was his boat anyway, and he was in charge. No one could do anything about it without his permission whatever Rowena thought.

Toby was jumping up and down. 'Let's go *now*. It won't hurt, will it, if we just go and see?'

Lynette got to her feet. 'Tomorrow will be better when we've got *Seaspray* too. We may have to look at all the islands. Much easier with two boats, and being able to signal to each other.'

Toby looked at her doubtfully. Lynette knew that sailing to the Mellon Isles had been his dream for days. The signalling had been his idea, too. He gave a little sigh, but then said no more.

Roddy nodded at Lynette, and then looked across at the islands. 'It's a mile across there, at least. Further to some of the other islands. We'll go tomorrow . . . if Mr Havill approves.'

Rowena flushed with indignation. 'You're not going to bring *Dad* into it? He's bound to stop us. Have some sense!'

Roddy shrugged, and started to walk back down the hill again. The boys followed, but Rowena glared at Lynette as if she knew how relieved she was that *Seaspray* was out of action today and so they couldn't go without permission.

'It's better, really,' Lynette began, but Rowena turned her back on her in disgust and went on ahead, doing a running limp down through the heather until she had overtaken the boys.

'Trust you to be so dismally goody-goody,' she shouted back. 'Spoiling everything.'

Lynette followed slowly. She knew she had sounded like that, but she hadn't meant it that way. She, as well as Roddy, was desperately keen to stop anyone taking away a very rare plant. But how were the five of them actually going to stop them? Certainly not by chasing them now because they could be miles away. Even if they weren't they'd see them coming.

Something of this had occurred to Neil by the time they all reached the beach. 'Your plan's rubbish,

Rowena. What's the good of letting them know we suspect them?'

Rowena stumped down to the water's edge, looking as if she intended to rush out through the water to *Shona* and take off after them on her own. But then she obviously thought better of it, and came back to the rocks. Even her back, as she sat there, looked angry. Lynette was reminded at once of that first evening in Uncle Alec's boat when they were coming back past Coronsay towing *Seaspray* and not knowing then how important their rescue of Rowena was going to prove.

Lynette sighed. Without that they might never have got the chance to sail, or to be here now quarrelling about what they would do next. Without it she might never have had the chance, either, of talking to Rowena and trying to help her. But it looked as if all that was gone now, driven out of Rowena's mind by her frustration at not being allowed to chase after the Rammers immediately. Family relations? What a laugh! Anyone could see that Neil and Rowena would never agree about anything.

Rowena picked up a stone and hurled it angrily into the sea as if she would like to do the same to her brother.

'What are we going to do now?' asked Toby.

'Best get back,' said Roddy. 'The paint should have hardened by now, and there might be something else to be done to it.'

He didn't say, but Lynette could well imagine, that he was tired of the bickering and wanted to be back in his workshop rather than here.

At six o'clock they all left the workshop to meet Mr Havill at the jetty. There were some explanations, but no one said that they had fallen out with Rowena, or that she had tried to get Roddy to go to the Mellon Isles against his better judgment. And when their proposed trip to the islands next day was raised Rowena seemed to take no interest.

Mr Havill looked enquiringly at Roddy. 'You're not already booked up tomorrow?'

'We said he wasn't,' Rowena said crossly.

Her father looked annoyed. 'Let the lad answer for himself. He may have other plans.'

Roddy hadn't, and said so. He also said that he was concerned about people digging up the roots of a rare plant, and wanted to see if they were at it over on the islands. He took no notice of Rowena's scowling face.

'Plants, is it?' said Mr Havill smiling. 'I thought fishing was more in your line? Or boat repairing. I'd like a look at ours if I may. And we'll settle up for the work you've put in.'

Rowena looked incensed. 'Settle up? What for? Roddy doesn't expect to be *paid*! We're all in this together, aren't we Roddy? Go on, tell him.'

'Aye.' Roddy squared his shoulders, his eyes glinting.

'I shall pay for your materials, Roddy,' Mr Havill said. 'But I'd be happier giving you some sort of reward for all the hard work you've put in, as well.'

'Reward?' cried Neil. 'All he wants is to stop people stealing.'

His father laughed. 'I'm not doing that, surely?'

'Not *you* Dad. We're not blaming you.'

'That's nice to know.' The spark of humour in his voice faded as he glanced at Rowena. 'We're off climbing again tomorrow, your mother and I.' He looked back at Roddy, smiling again. 'And we're grateful to you, lad, for looking after our two for us.'

Rowena scowled, but Neil laughed.

From the end of the jetty Lynette watched the exchange between them. Neil and his father were so alike. Even the way they were standing with heads thrown back and feet slightly apart as if they couldn't wait to get moving on some activity or other. There seemed to be a special relationship between them which excluded Rowena. Lynette felt a stab of sympathy for her.

'Anyway, have a good day out with this lot,' Mr Havill said. 'Are Lynette and Toby going too?'

Toby, rather red in the face with enthusiasm, said they wanted to, more than anything.

'You can have a lift with us to the cottage now if you like,' said Mr Havill. 'And then you can clear it with your uncle. What's more, I'll pick you up and drive you to Butallie tomorrow if he agrees.'

The tide was going out, and the sharp smell of uncovered seaweed stung their nostrils next morning as *Seaspray* was brought down to the water on Roddy's launching trolley.

It was a big moment, and Toby had eyes for nothing else as the trolley was pushed into the water alongside the jetty and the dinghy floated off it very gently. Toby helped Roddy haul the trolley back onto dry land to be parked nearby.

He knew that he and Lynette would be in *Shona* with Roddy, but all the same he couldn't help his disappointment showing in his expression as the two boats set out from Butallie. Toby would have loved to sail *Seaspray* again.

With the slight breeze dead astern *Seaspray* was making slow progress, and he could see Rowena's frustration as she tilted the boat one way and then the other, hoping, he knew, to catch what little wind there was.

'We'll never get there at this rate,' Toby mumbled to himself.

Lynette, seated in the bows, gazed down through the still water to the ridged sand beneath. The land behind them was slightly hazy.

Roddy stood at the tiller, his khaki bush hat as usual well back on his head. He stared around, frowning, the sunshine on his tanned face highlighting his prominent features. He looked a force to be reckoned with if they were fortunate enough to meet the Rammers today. Lynette smiled at him, but he didn't smile back. She knew he was too engrossed in their plans, and didn't mind.

Her rucksack was at her feet, bulging with all the things she thought they might need for a long day in the islands. Uncle Alec had given her a large scale map of them he'd made himself when he was a boy.

'So you know what they're like?' she had asked him as soon as Mr Havill and the others had left the cottage yesterday. Everyone had been so full of all they were going to do that she suspected that Uncle Alec would have liked to come too. He had joked with them later, saying that it would keep them out of mischief discovering plant thieves.

'But that's why we're going,' Toby had said indignantly.

'Aye, smugglers, plant thieves, pirates . . .'

Lynette had sighed. He never took anything they planned with the seriousness they felt it deserved, especially in this case. But now, in *Shona* on this peacefully quiet day, she could hardly believe that anything was going to happen at all.

Suddenly there were raised voices from *Seaspray*. Glancing back at them, Lynette saw Rowena rise to her feet, and then sink down again. Neil, red-faced, looked as if he would like to hit her.

'What's up?' Roddy called back to her.

Before she could say anything Lynette gave a gasp. 'Look, over there!'

She could see a tiny speck in the distance. The boat didn't change course but kept going towards the islands until it was out of sight.

Roddy pushed the throttle forward and *Shona* leapt ahead. But the other boat had vanished as if it had never been. Disappointed, Roddy brought *Shona* round in a wide arc and back to *Seaspray*.

'Want a tow?' he called to them. 'We think we've seen them.'

Normally Rowena would have refused in indignation, but now she nodded. 'Toby can come aboard here instead of me,' she said. 'I've had enough.'

Without a word Roddy brought *Shona* alongside the sailing dinghy, and the changes were made. With the tow rope in position they made greater speed. They moved towards the Mellon Isles, all of them looking hard ahead.

Chapter Eleven

The islands looked close now, and there were dark patches on the sea that meant wind was coming.

'Stand by to loosen the tow rope,' Roddy called out.

Neil waved, and moved forward. On *Shona* Rowena pulled the rope aboard and coiled it neatly. Then Roddy opened the throttle again. 'Catch us up as soon as you can,' he shouted.

For answer came two seagull calls.

'*Message received,*' Lynette murmured. She glanced back at *Seaspray* where Neil had tightened the mainsail. Both boys were sitting up on one side now the wind had strenghtened. She felt a thrill of excitement as the gap widened between them.

'That's Mellera More,' said Roddy. He waved one arm at a solid mass of land ahead bordered with dark cliffs. It was rimmed by yellow and brown seaweed as the tide fell. 'It's the only island with a name. Someone lived there years ago.'

Lynette looked at the lonely landscape with awe as they moved along towards it.

Roddy slowed the engine. 'Best wait for the others now,' he said. 'We'll have to separate and go in different directions or we've no hope of finding anything.

As soon as *Seaspray* came close he shouted his orders. 'Signal if you see anything suspicious,' he called after them.

'Like what?' Rowena muttered at his side.

Roddy, staring ahead, didn't answer. They were going along by the edge of another island, whose cliffs were nearly as steep as those of Mellera More which they would soon reach. To her surprise Lynette saw a narrow gap between the two islands. As Roddy steered *Shona* through she gave a gasp of delight. It was a different world in here in which sunlight rippled on an inland sea dotted with small heathery islands.

'It doesn't look as if anyone ever comes here,' she said.

'Sometimes sheep are brought across for the summer months,' Roddy said.

'Sheep?'

'Aye, for grazing. We'll look round here first, and work our way round Mellera More. Then we'll search the ruined house there.'

Ahead was a rocky beach bounded by grassy slopes with a hill rising behind. *Shona* was moving slowly now, and except for the engine there was no sound. The sun was hot on their faces.

'Listen!' said Rowena suddenly.

Roddy stopped the engine. Lynette's heart seemed to leap into her throat at the unmistakable sound of another engine. It was hard to tell at first where the sound was coming from, but then they saw the boat coming through the gap they had used only moments before. The man and woman in it were talking earnestly, and taking no notice of them at all. Could it be they hadn't seen them?

All three in *Shona* froze. Even Rowena said nothing until the other boat had moved out of sight behind an island no bigger than a heather-covered rock.

'After them!' she hissed as the boat reappeared, going away fast. She shouted something else but her voice was lost in the burst from *Shona*'s engine. The sound changed suddenly, and *Shona* jerked almost to a stop.

'What's wrong?' Rowena cried.

Roddy, leaning over the stern, didn't answer. He was trying hard to disentangle the propeller. 'Seaweed,' he said in disgust. 'A whole mass of it. We went into it like fools, right enough.'

Now they were looking they could see thick brown seaweed like an oil slick on the calm water. Roddy tore at it furiously, helped by Rowena.

'Just when we could have got them,' she cried.

'We saw where they went,' said Lynette. 'And there's clear water ahead.'

'We've got to beach *Shona* to make sure the propeller's free of it,' Roddy said. He reached for an oar, and stood in the stern to push the oar into the seaweed. With deft strokes he moved the boat towards the beach of the other island.

'There's sand beneath us now,' said Lynette. 'I can see huge scallop shells down there, and . . .' she broke off, white-faced. '*Bones!*'

Rowena leapt across the boat to look.

'Sheep bones,' said Roddy briefly as he pulled the oar in. He leapt over the side, thigh-deep in water, to examine the propeller. 'Get out and give me a hand,' he said to Rowena. 'Hold it steady, Lynette.'

As *Shona* moved nearer the beach Lynette scrambled out too, and then gave a muffled gasp as she saw more bones lying on the sand. She kicked one away, remembering Uncle Alec's joke on their first day about their own bones lying bleached on the sand of Coronsay if he forgot to come back for them after attending to his lobster pots.

Toby and Neil, in *Seaspray*, were doing as Roddy had said and circumnavigating the islands in the other direction. The sun cast intermittent shadows on the land as they passed, and the sea changed swiftly from deep purple to turquoise as great clouds moved across the sky.

Once they caught sight of another boat, but to their disappointment it was making for Butallie on the mainland and was obviously one of the larger fishing vessels. After that it seemed that *Seaspray* was the only boat in the world.

'If only the Rammers would come nosing round *now*!' said Toby. 'We'd get them for sure.'

Neil had his camera ready just in case, and Toby looked at him scornfully. 'What's the use of that? You'd be wasting time. We've got to act fast when we see them.'

'Proof,' said Neil. 'We might need proof.'

'And let them get away?'

Neil took no notice. He shrugged, and raised his camera to look through the viewfinder.

'Let me helm,' Toby demanded. 'I know what to do.'

Neil stayed where he was with one hand resting lightly on the tiller and with his camera held to his eyes with the other.

Toby muttered something. It wasn't fair. Neil ought to give him a chance. He'd never get any practice at helming at this rate. While they were waiting for the Rammers was as good a time as any, but all Neil could think of was his precious camera.

'Toby!' Neil cried so loudly and suddenly that Toby jumped round in surprise. 'Look, there's Lynette on that hill. Can you see her?'

Lynette was leaping up and down, frantically waving and screaming out seagull signals.

Toby was busy counting. 'Six. *Come here at once.* They've seen the Rammers!'

As Lynette came flying down the hill to meet them Neil brought *Seaspray* as close to the rocky shore as he dared. Lynette was gasping so much she could hardly speak, and they had to wait a few seconds while she took several deep breaths.

'Round the other side,' she got out at last. 'We saw

them, but they didn't see us. At least we don't think so. Roddy wants you to come.'

Neil looked worried. 'We can't land here.'

'Go back the way you've come. There's a gap between the islands, but be careful. The propeller got fouled in a mass of horrid thick seaweed. There's a beach you can land on. You'll see it easily. But be *quick!*'

She leapt away, and was soon up the hill again and out of sight.

Neil put his camera away at once, and now even Toby couldn't complain that he was wasting time. They tacked backwards and forwards against the rising breeze to get back to where they had left the others. Neil's orders were as crisp as Rowena's would have been. Toby fidgeted impatiently as he watched out for the gap between the islands. At last he caught sight of it.

As soon as they were through they saw *Shona* moored near the beach and the others there waiting for them.

Neil remembered the warning about the lethal seaweed. 'Get the paddle out,' he ordered. He pulled the rudder up out of the way, and leaned forward to raise the centreboard. With Toby working hard with the paddle *Seaspray* moved through the ugly brown mass fairly easily.

Roddy strode into the water to meet them, and to help haul *Seaspray* on to the beach. He looked fiercely determined.

'Those people – I've seen them before.'

'Where?' Toby cried. 'Where did you see them? Can we go after them?'

'We know where they went,' said Lynette. 'It took ages to clear the propeller. That's why we're here on Falcon Island. That's its name now.'

Rowena scowled at Roddy. 'We're wasting time.'

'Who are they, Roddy?' Toby asked impatiently.

'The woman's called Marise Brown. They were in Butallie last week staying in Mrs Crawford's cottage.

It's them, right enough.'

Toby looked triumphant. 'Come on then! Let's do something.'

'We'll go after them of course!' This from Rowena who was already moving down the beach.'

'Wait!' Roddy's voice was stern, and she paused and looked round. 'There's a small landing place on the other side of the big island, Mellera More. That's where they're going, sure enough. We'll give them time to land and move off before we go after them or they'll see us.'

'That's important,' Lynette agreed, remembering Uncle Alec's jokes. The only way to make him take it seriously was to find proof of what those people were doing to convince him to do something about it. 'Roddy's right,' she said earnestly.

'How much time?' Toby demanded.

Rowena tossed her dark head. 'Don't be dismal, Roddy. We need action now.'

'We do not.'

'That was the boat that tried to wreck *Seaspray*, and they're not going to get away with it. I'll go after them by myself.'

Roddy stiffened for a moment, and then was after her in great angry strides as she rushed towards *Seaspray*. The dinghy was leaning to one side, red sails flapping. Roddy reached inside and grabbed the tiller. He turned to face her, his face set in determined lines.

'*Seaspray*'s ours,' Rowena burst out. 'I'll sail if I want to, and you can't stop me!'

Roddy looked as if he would hit her with the tiller. She stepped back a pace as the others came to them.

'We're all in this together,' Lynette cried. 'All of us. We've got to do it properly. I'm not sure we shouldn't go back to the mainland and get Uncle Alec if we're sure it was those people who tried to push *Seaspray* onto the rocks.'

There was a howl of protest from Neil and Toby.

'If it's just revenge you want, Rowena . . .' Roddy began.

Lynette looked at her earnestly. 'We all belong together against the Rammers, Rowena.'

'Not only revenge,' Rowena muttered.

'What then?' Roddy looked at her keenly, and a lot seemed to hang on her answer.

'I want the same as you . . . To get proof of what they're doing.'

Roddy's face relaxed, and he smiled. 'Right enough.'

Neil glanced up at *Seaspray*'s red sails conspicuous against the sand and sea. 'Why don't we hide *Seaspray* on this island, and all of us go after them in *Shona*?'

'Good sense,' said Roddy. 'Rowena?'

She nodded, thinking hard. 'Behind those rocks? Come on, everybody, get moving.'

She looked happier now as if something important had been resolved, and threw herself with enthusiasm into the combined action needed to take down the sails and dismast the boat. Lynette and Neil folded the sails and pushed them hurriedly into the sail bag. That, and the three orange life-jackets, were thrust inside the lockers. The rucksack and the Havills' bag of food were removed to take with them in *Shona*, and Neil made sure his camera was safely in position on the strap round his neck.

The hull was turned upside down and carried further up to the soft sand and placed behind the rocks where it lay gleaming like a freshly beached whale.

Rowena frowned at it. 'That's no good. It shows up far too much.'

'Let's cover it with sand and seaweed,' Lynette suggested, earning a nod of approval from Rowena.

They all grabbed handfuls of sand to throw on it, and Neil and Toby collected armfuls of soggy brown weed to drape over the top. The mast and boom were covered in sand too.

For a moment they all stood admiring the transformation. Then they ran down to the water's edge.

Chapter Twelve

'Toby, you're smallest. Out you get,' Roddy ordered. 'You'll need to climb up the hill a bit. See if their boat's at the landing stage. We can't risk going round in *Shona*.'

Toby leapt ashore nimbly on Mellera More, and was off at once clambering away out of sight. They were in a small inlet bounded by rocks and overhanging turf. It was the best place Roddy could find for leaving *Shona* if they intended to land. He fixed the anchor on the turf in readiness, and then let *Shona* drift out a little to the end of the rope. Neil wrinkled his nose as the bitter seaweed smell reached him.

'The tide's on the ebb,' Roddy said. 'She'll take no harm for a while.'

All four of them sat motionless, listening. At last came a single seagull call. *Attention*!

Rowena raised her face. 'He's found something!'

Toby came bounding down over the rough ground towards them. 'Their boat's there,' he said quickly. 'I saw it tied to the jetty. I saw the house too. There's no sign of anyone, though.'

'Right,' said Roddy. There was a determined gleam in his eyes as he stood up to pull *Shona* nearer to shore. 'The rocks are a bit tricky to climb over. Can you manage, Rowena?'

Her dark eyes sparkled, and her cheeks glowed as she rolled up the legs of her jeans. 'Just try me!'

Toby could hardly keep still. From his vantage point on dry ground he looked at the others in exasperation. It was taking them a long time to manoeuvre themselves across the slippery rocks and put their trainers back on. Too long, when there was plenty to be done.

'Come on,' he called urgently. This was the most adventurous thing he'd ever been involved in, and he didn't want to lose a second of it.

'Now what?' Neil asked when they were all ready.

Roddy squared his shoulders, and made sure his bush hat was firmly in position. 'The house . . . they'll likely be there. We'll need to take a look at it. Keep your heads down.'

Near the brow of the higher ground they threw themselves down, and wriggled up the rest of the way through the pungent heather. Neil sneezed twice. Lynette's rucksack caught in the stiff stems and pulled her back. She took precious seconds to extricate it, and was the last to reach the top.

'There's the house,' Toby whispered. 'They're in there. They must be.'

Lynette had a moment's doubt. The house looked deserted in its peaceful green setting. The front door and five empty windows stared sightlessly out to sea. Heather-covered ground rose to the sky behind the broken roof. On the windowless side nearest to them were dilapidated outbuildings half-hidden in bushes.

'D'you think they'll come out soon?' Neil asked hopefully as he propped himself up on his elbows for a better view.

'We'll give them fifteen minutes,' said Roddy. 'Then we'll start a search.'

Toby couldn't help wriggling a little. He glanced at his watch, and then shook it in case the hands had stopped. The ticking was loud in the tense silence.

They could see a long way around them, not only the house but over to the other islands in the group as well. Lynette leaned against her rucksack, careful to keep her head low.

'It's really beautiful,' she said.

But the others weren't interested in scenery. Neil moved a little to get comfortable.

'Keep down,' Rowena hissed. She was looking this way and that, moving the heather aside every now and again to take another look at the silent house.

Roddy was deep in thought, and sitting motionless with his hands on his knees. With his khaki hat on his head he was the most camouflaged so that if he had been bobbing about like Toby no one would have known he was there watching for something to happen.

'It's easy to believe in God when you see all these lovely islands and the heather and the smooth sea and everything,' Lynette murmured dreamily.

'No one said it wasn't,' Rowena retorted.

Neil rolled over and looked at his sister, but she only glared at him and he turned away again. 'I know what you mean,' he said. 'Miles and miles of it. It wasn't just an accident. Someone must have made it in the beginning. And us, too.'

Lynette held her breath. She hadn't meant to speak aloud just then. It was what she was thinking. How could anyone see the mountains fading into the mauve distance and hear the sea birds calling, and see the wild flowers and butterflies without believing in God?

'Aye,' said Roddy without moving. 'We have a responsibility towards it, right enough.'

Lynette knew he was thinking of Coronsay.

'Responsibility?' Rowena demanded. 'It's easy enough looking after *places*. They can't answer back or say what they want for themselves. But with people its different. And life. It just isn't fair.'

Toby wriggled closer. 'It's not easy to look after places, or the Rammers wouldn't have been allowed to dig up the plants in the first place.'

95

'Who would stop them? No one saw, except us. That's why we're here, stupid.'

'Don't call him stupid,' Neil said indignantly. 'Life would be butterflies and dandelions if it wasn't for people like you.'

'What's that supposed to mean?'

Neil shrugged. 'How should I know? I just said it.'

But Lynette thought it sounded real as if he'd read it somewhere and remembered.

'Life is what we make it, with God's help,' Roddy said sternly.

'That's what Dad says,' said Toby. 'He says we have to do our best in the situation we find ourselves in. We must love others like we love ourselves.'

'And love God, and ask him for the help we need,' Lynette said quickly.

She glanced at Rowena whose scoffing reply was drowned in a cry from Toby. 'Look!'

'Keep down,' Roddy warned, only just in time.

A boat was coming across the glassy sea with three people in it. Were they more people coming to join the others, or nothing to do with them at all? More important, would they see *Shona* moored in the small inlet and know that someone else was here too?

They watched, tense and silent, expecting the boat to alter course and go straight to *Shona*'s hiding place. But it came straight for the jetty.

A click from Neil's camera was the only sound on the hill.

'They know what they're doing,' Roddy said quietly. 'They're tying up to the other boat.'

'So they know them,' Toby said in excitement. 'They're in the same gang.'

'But it doesn't prove anything,' said Lynette. She wished it did, and then they could return to the mainland in *Shona* at once before anyone knew they were here. Now she could see them these people were real, and the situation seemed rather frightening. Please help us, God, she prayed silently. Please keep us safe. Amen.

Even though they had been talking about God she couldn't suggest they should pray together. Dad would have done so at once, and it would have been perfectly natural.

She could feel the tenseness about the others as they stared at the two men and a girl walking up the beach towards the house. They moved purposely, the men in high sea boots and the girl's brown cords tucked into grey socks. She wore dirty trainers. Her long brown hair was pulled back from her face.

Toby moved and Lynette clutched his arm. Neil was clicking away with his camera. She wished they were safely away, but what good would that do? No use at all to return to Butallie to say that they had seen three men and two women on Mellera More and thought they were up to something. They would deserve Uncle Alec's jokes about bandits if they couldn't discover for themselves what these people were doing.

As soon as the rickety door of the house slammed behind the three of them Toby leapt up.

'Get *down*!' Roddy commanded. 'There are five of them . . .'

'And five of us!' Rowena's eyes gleamed. 'We've found their headquarters and . . .' She broke off as the door opened again and a man and woman came out.

Roddy grabbed Rowena and held her down or she would have leapt up in fury wanting to level the score with them immediately for the damage they had done to her boat.

It was the hardest thing in the world for them to keep still and not give themselves away. The two people seemed to know they were being watched as they walked around the house looking up at the higher ground surrounding it. After a while though they seemed satisfied, but instead of going back inside the house they began to walk up the hill behind it. They seemed to take ages to get to the top even though it wasn't far.

'Now what?' Neil whispered when they couldn't be seen any longer.

For a moment Roddy seemed undecided. They all looked at him expectantly, Rowena and Toby ready to spring into action, Neil looking interested and Lynette doubtful.

'Wait here,' he said, making up his mind suddenly. 'I'll signal if I see anything. We need to know the coast's clear. I'll not be long.'

He was off at once, and even though they knew where he was he was difficult to see.

'You can tell his dad taught him stalking,' Toby said admiringly. 'Look he's there already . . . over there and moving up the hill!'

Roddy going off on his own made good sense, but at least two of the watchers on the hill felt aggrieved. By the stiffness of Toby's shoulders Lynette knew he was disappointed not to be going too.

'Look,' Neil whispered. 'They're coming back . . . making straight for the house.'

Had they seen Roddy? It seemed not for they walked unconcernedly and went inside, shutting the door behind them. For a few moments they all stared at the house, but there was no sign of movement inside. Anyone would think it was completely deserted if they didn't know any better.

To their surprise Roddy was back before they knew it. He pulled his hat forward as he got down beside them.

'They didn't see me!' The excitement in his voice told them at once that something was afoot. 'Come on, all of you, but be careful. There's something interesting you've got to see.'

Chapter Thirteen

At once Roddy was off ahead of them, taking them round the hill this time instead of over the top. They were all breathless by the time Roddy stopped.

'Look!' he said.

They stared in astonishment at the large patch of cleared ground in front of them, and at the rows and rows of small plants growing there.

With a cry Lynette ran forward, throwing herself down on her knees. There were no flowers, but the spiky leaves were familiar. 'Coronwort,' she said, her voice trembling. 'I'm certain of it.'

Rowena sounded angry. 'But *why*?'

'We need to find that out, right enough,' Roddy said grimly. 'Then we'll go straight back to the mainland and report it.'

Neil held his camera in position to take a photograph. 'I've only got two left now,' he said in dismay.

'All these plants,' Lynette said in wonder as she stood up and brushed down the knees of her jeans. 'They've been growing them here on Mellera More, and they didn't want anyone to know.'

'Come on,' said Roddy. He looked round as if he expected the truth to materialise on the surrounding hillside. 'We'll need to look further. Inside the house, maybe.'

'*Inside* the house?' Toby asked, his eyes round.

'Aye, if we want to find out what they're doing with

these plants. They're not growing them for flower arranging that's for sure.'

Lynette looked concerned. 'But . . . should we?'

'Of course. Don't be dismal.' Rowena looked back over her shoulder. 'How else can we find out? Who'd take any notice of us if we go back saying we saw rows of growing plants?'

Not Uncle Alec for sure. Lynette saw that only too well. 'You promise we'll go straight back when we discover something?'

'Aye.' Roddy's eyes glinted with determination.

Lynette cast a backward look at the neat rows of coronwort as she followed the others back the way they had come. Whatever she had expected to find here on Mellera More it wasn't this. She tried hard to feel brave. It was one thing spying on the Rammers in the open air, another to follow them inside the house.

Roddy, in the lead as they topped the hill to look down again on the house, stopped suddenly. 'Get down!' he hissed.

As she fell to the ground Rowena let out a strangled cry. Her white face stared back at the others as she clutched her ankle.

'What's wrong now?' Neil whispered impatiently.

Rowena bent her dark head over her foot and said nothing. Lynette, down at her side, tried to see what was wrong. Neil hesitated for a moment, and then followed the other two as they wriggled forward to get a view of the house that looked so innocent in the sunshine.

'They're coming out,' Toby called back to them in a low voice that trembled with excitement. 'Three of them. They're going the other way, down to their jetty.'

But Lynette could think only of Rowena. 'Is it bad? Can you move it at all?'

'It's hurt – badly, I think.'

It was already swelling. Rowena tried to move it, and

gasped.

'It needs a bandage, a wet one tied tightly round,' said Lynette as she glanced round helplessly. All she could see was heather and rough grass as they all crouched down at the top of the hill. *Shona* was some way away, too far for Rowena to hobble to even with help. She didn't know what to do.

'The other two,' came Neil's loud whisper. 'I can see them. They're following the others to the jetty.'

'Now's our chance,' Roddy said firmly.

'But we can't,' said Lynette in anguish. 'It's getting worse every minute. Rowena can't walk . . .'

Roddy glanced back at her, frowning. 'We need a look-out here – you, Rowena. Seagull-signal at once if you see anything.'

'Come *on*!' Toby said, already moving forward.

Lynette took a deep breath. 'I'll stay with her.'

'No, you come with us.'

Roddy looked so fierce she dared not argue, and followed the boys down the hill to the bushes at the back of the house that half-covered an outhouse. Inside the cool ruined building they huddled together, expecting the Rammers to return and find them at any moment. Grass and rank weeds clung to the base of the damp walls. Lynette shivered.

The back of the house hadn't fallen into the same disrepair as the front. There was even glass in the downstairs windows. Roddy stepped out of the shelter of the outhouse, and felt the back door handle. It turned, but nothing happened. He stared up at the top windows. Climbing up to them would be impossible. He returned to the others deep in thought.

'Let's try the front,' Toby said, his eyes round with excitement.

'It's risky,' said Neil eagerly, his eyes shining in the gloom.

Roddy's eyebrows contracted as he thought hard.

Then he pulled a crumpled grey rag from his pocket. 'We'll split up. Three of us to get inside the house through the broken windows at the front, Neil, Toby and me. One of us will come out at once with this rag dampened for Rowena.' He looked speculatively at Lynette. 'Take it up to her and stay there. Someone will stay out here to keep watch, and to relay any seagull-signal from the hill.'

'What are we waiting for?' Toby demanded, standing on first one foot and then the other.

Lynette shuddered. She didn't like this one little bit, and the sooner it was over the better.

'Right then.' Roddy pulled his hat down hard on his head as if it would make him invisible. 'I'll check it's safe.' He went outside and, keeping close to the wall, peered round the corner of the house. 'All clear!'

'Good luck,' Lynette whispered.

The two boys were beside him in an instant.

At the front of the house Roddy raised his head to look through the broken glass of the window. 'I'm going inside,' he said. 'Follow me as soon as I'm in, but be careful.'

When Neil joined the other two Roddy was at the door into the passage, listening hard. It squeaked a little as he opened it. He tried two other doors, and then shut them again.

'What are you looking for?' asked Toby.

'Water.'

The third door he opened led into a dilapidated kitchen whose dripping tap made him exclaim in relief. Seconds later Toby was climbing out through the window again with the soaking rag clutched in his hand.

Lynette was relieved to see him and took it from him quickly. 'Are Roddy and Neil all right?'

Toby nodded without speaking, and she knew it was because he was disappointed at being banished out here to keep watch instead of taking part in more dangerous activities inside the house. Rowena would have enjoyed it, too. Lynette wished she could have changed places with her. Rowena was the right person for such a dangerous operation, but instead she had to be left behind on the lonely hill. Even worse for her than Toby.

Carefully she slipped outside the crumbling building, but then hesitated and looked back. 'Will you be all right, Toby?'

'Of course,' he said crossly. 'Take care they don't see *you*.'

Lynette shivered as she started on her way. Her heart was thudding so much she could hardly breathe.

Rowena, alone on her hill, had plenty of time to think. Now that the others had disappeared she had no idea of what was going on, and she didn't like it. She was here to keep a look-out, but there wasn't the slightest movement apart from the wind in her hair each time she raised her head to look around. Anyone would think the house had never been lived in. It looked as if someone had found a ruined house somewhere and plonked it down on the only green patch of grass in the islands to get rid of it.

She thumped the ground with her hand until it hurt. To have this happen at the very worst moment. It simply wasn't fair! Scowling, she straightened her leg to try to ease her swollen ankle. Why did this have to happen to her, anyway? She was the one who wanted to get at the Rammers for the harm they had tried to do to *Seaspray* and for stealing from Coronsay. She had urged action from the beginning when Lynette was anxious to avoid any confrontation that might cause trouble. And now here she was, stuck on top of a hill and the others were having all the fun. It simply wasn't fair!

If only she knew what was going on inside the house! She raised her head again, and stared at it as if it was all she needed to do to start some action. The land on the other side looked dark and brooding now that clouds covered the sun. There was a heaviness over everything that hadn't been there when they had landed on Mellera More. Even the grey sea looked less friendly.

She flopped down again. A bee buzzed round her hair and she waved it away angrily. It was agony not knowing what was happening. And her ankle hurt, badly. No way was *she* going to manage to get back to *Shona* when it was time to go, but no one cared. No one at all.

Not a movement . . . not a sound either now the seagulls were silent. She had never felt so alone in all her life. It seemed to go on for ever, the heathery ground, the outcrops of rock, the other islands, the sea . . . The intense silence pricked her ears, and the limitless space stretching around her hurt her eyes.

What was she going to do . . . what *could* she do with an ankle that already looked like a balloon? And what would Dad say when the others went back without her and she had to be rescued again?

But this time it wasn't her own fault. No one could blame her for coming to Mellera More today with Roddy and the others because it had all been planned. Not like last time when she had gone off sailing on her own in a temper with Neil, determined to show him. Show him what – that she couldn't cope on her own as well as she thought and had to be rescued by that man in front of those two children?

Rowena opened her eyes, and stared at a twig of heather, thinking about Lynette and Toby. How they must have laughed about her afterwards and the stupid way she had let their uncle carry her down to be refloated in *Seaspray*. Who wanted to be rescued by a couple of kids? But had they laughed at her behind her back? This was the first time such a thought had entered her head, and it took her by surprise. Maybe Toby was so envious of her boat he hadn't even thought of it.

Maybe Lynette had other things to think about.

Nothing was different . . . the same rocky ground, the same sea and cloudy sky. But something had happened. She wasn't angry any more. That was different. But she was still alone on the hill, and her ankle still hurt.

Chapter Fourteen

Rowena turned suddenly, awakened out of her reverie by the swish of the heather as Lynette crawled through it to reach her.

Lynette looked at her anxiously. 'Is it any worse? I've brought a wet rag to use as a bandage. It needs to go on tightly.'

Rowena flushed, and there was a suspicious dampness about her eyes. 'For me . . . you got it for me?'

'Roddy got Toby to wet it at a tap in the house. Hurry, the sooner it's on the better.'

Rowena took it and wound it round her swollen ankle, wincing a little as she pulled it tight. 'What's going on? Has anything happened? Have you seen anyone? I haven't. At least . . .' She broke off awkwardly. 'I've been thinking, you see.'

Lynette settled herself comfortably. 'About what we'll do next?'

'No. Not that. Something else. Something different . . .' She broke off, and Lynette saw that her face was pale again now.

She looked at her anxiously. 'Are you all right? I'm sorry I left you on your own, but Roddy . . .'

'I'm all right. But the boys . . .'

'Toby's mad because he's got to wait for the others outside the house. Roddy and Neil are inside now.' Lynette raised her head and parted the heather a little so she could see the back of the house. 'With luck the

Rammers will keep right away until the boys get out. I wish they'd hurry.'

Rowena moved her foot a little. 'About what you said on our first day on Coronsay. What did you mean when you said God is always with you?'

For a moment Lynette said nothing. Not because it wasn't true, but because she was afraid of saying the wrong thing. It was the opportunity she had been praying for. Rowena had asked her the question, but suppose her answer put her off? She took a deep breath. 'I feel that God is always there taking care of me,' she said at last.

Rowena kept silent, and it was worse than if she had lashed out with some bitter remark that she might have been able to answer.

'I mean,' Lynette said, floundering. 'I mean . . . you see it feels as if God cares as he cares for everyone if we ask him into our lives.'

Rowena stared at her swollen ankle, her head bent.

Lynette closed her eyes and began to pray hard. 'Please God, help me.' Be specific, Dad always said, and she had been, hadn't she? 'Please God help me to help Rowena to love you . . . somehow. Please help so I know what to say.'

Rowena raised her head, and her eyes looked unhappy. 'I don't even *look* like them.'

'Who?'

'The rest of my family.'

'But do you have to? Lots of families don't look alike. You seem like a Havill to me.'

'And to God? Don't give me any rubbish about being in God's family. I want to belong to the Havill family.'

'But you *are* as well! God cares for you like your own father . . .'

'Dad!' Rowena exclaimed. 'Don't mention Dad. 'He doesn't care about *me* one little bit.'

'So why was he angry when Uncle Alec brought you

back to the harbour that first night? Your dad wouldn't have been angry if he didn't care what happened to you . . .'

Rowena caught hold of her arm with a suddenness that made Lynette jump. Over on the other side of the house two people appeared on the brow of the hill. They were standing still and looking around them.

'Have they seen *Shona*?' Lynette whispered, her heart thudding.

Rowena's voice shook. 'Yes, I think they have. They're pointing. They're moving!'

'This way? No, thank goodness. They're going to the coronwort place.' Lynette felt light-headed with relief as they vanished over the skyline. They might so easily have gone to the house first.

'We forgot to signal,' Rowena said, aghast.

'It wouldn't have helped,' Lynette said quickly. 'Not in this case. The Rammers are out of sight now.'

Rowena moved her position so that she was lying face down and peering intently through the gap she had made in the heather. 'Stand by to seagull-signal the minute they come back. Something'll happen soon!' Her voice rang with excitement, and her body stiffened.

Lynette sighed. It was too late to talk now. Rowena was no longer interested. But she had asked God's help in reaching her, hadn't she? She had to trust that her prayer was already being answered.

Inside the house, Roddy and Neil crept cautiously along the passage to the room at the back next to the kitchen that they had already seen. For a tense moment they listened outside the closed door, and then Roddy turned the handle and they slipped inside.

At first they could see nothing because of the black curtains across the window that let in only a chink of light. But soon, as their eyes became accustomed to the gloom, they stared in amazement at the piles of small plants all packaged tightly in polythene bags.

'. . . Hundreds of them,' Neil whispered, his eyes round. 'It's coronwort . . . masses and masses of coronwort.'

Roddy picked up a packet and slipped it into the back pocket of his jeans. 'We'll need to get back, fast.'

'Wait. I'll take a photo,' Neil said.

Roddy patted his pocket. 'Here's proof enough.'

'Anyone can package plants they've grown themselves.'

'Not this one. They've pillaged Coronsay.' Roddy's voice was grim.

Neil knew better than to argue. 'Let's look in the other room first,' he said.

In here were piles of small boxes, some packed into larger ones. One, full of dry petals, lay open.

Roddy gave a low whistle. 'It's a factory line for something, right enough.'

Neil picked up one of the other boxes and shook it. 'It's light, but it's full of something. Petal dust?'

'Someone will know what it's about,' Roddy said triumphantly as he took it from him and put it in his pocket with the plant. 'Come on. Let's go.'

They slipped into the passage, and stopped dead at a sudden rattling noise.

'It's only the wind,' Neil whispered. 'It's getting rough.'

They risked using the front door. For a moment they stood flat against the outside wall of the house, and then made quickly for the outhouse at the back where Toby was waiting.

'We found enough to get them,' Neil cried, his eyes shining.

Roddy was poised for action. 'Any signals, Toby?'

Toby shook his head. 'I thought you'd never come. Back to *Shona* now then. Who'll fetch the girls?'

On his way out Roddy paused and looked round.

'Rowena will stay where she is.'

Neil was appalled. 'Leave her here alone on Mellera More with the Rammers? No way.'

'She'll be safe if she keeps hidden.'

'You know Rowena.' Neil's face was flushed. 'If they come close . . . I can't leave her . . .'

Four seagull cries rent the air. They looked at each other, alarmed. Another four calls, then another. *Danger. Danger. Danger.* Seagull signals, not the real thing.

'Keep back!' Roddy hissed. He poked his head very gingerly round the door frame of the outhouse. 'I'm going to see.'

He was back almost at once. 'Two people are on the hillside between here and where we left *Shona*,' he reported. 'They're sitting down, keeping watch for us by the look of it. So they know we're on Mellera More. We'll not get past them unseen. The other three are coming back to the house. Come on!'

'But where?' Toby whispered.

Roddy frowned, the lines deep on his forehead. He had to make up his mind quickly. The other two, knowing this, stared at him expectantly.

'*Shona*'s no use now,' he said, in a tight voice. 'We need *Seaspray* for this.'

'But *Seaspray*'s hidden on Falcon Island,' Toby said.

Roddy looked at Neil. 'Are you a good swimmer, Neil? We'll need to swim for SEASPRAY, and bring her near to where the girls are. It's only narrow across there, but we'll have to land on rocks this side.' He looked at Toby. 'It has to be Neil. *Seaspray*'s his boat. With luck we'll all be away before they start searching for us. You'll need to get the girls down to the rocks ready for when we come.'

Toby nodded. He understood that.

'It'll not be easy,' Roddy warned, still frowning. 'Take it slowly, Toby. Lucky it's windy. Any noise you make 'won't be too obvious, but be careful.'

Toby didn't need to be told. He waited until first Roddy and then Neil had scooted across the open space to where the heather started at the bottom of the look-out hill. Then, very carefully, he eased his way out of the smelly outhouse. Keeping close to the wall of the house until the last minute he sprinted across too, hoping the Rammers were looking the other way. It wasn't until he reached the safety of the bitter-smelling heather that he paused to look back.

On the other hillside the two watchers were intent on something in the direction of the jetty. He hoped desperately that Roddy and Neil hadn't been seen as they wriggled their way down to the shore. Suppose one of the Rammers planned to intercept Roddy and Neil as they swam across the narrow channel? But no more seagull signals had been made, so with luck all was well.

Carefully he made his way up the hill for the second time. The hard heather stalks scratched his face, and he brushed them away so impatiently that one sprang back and hit him. He let out a muffled 'Oww!' and then lay still. Had anyone heard him? Cautiously he raised his head. He couldn't see the Rammers now, but that didn't necessarily mean anything. He couldn't see any sign of the girls, either, which was more worrying. He was near enough to the summit for them to have heard his involuntary cry.

The grey sky above him darkened as the first drops of rain fell.

Chapter Fifteen

Rowena shook her head and droplets of heavy rain sprayed her shoulders, and darkened her T-shirt. Lynette moved uncomfortably, and then moved back to the place she had vacated because the ground there was drier.

'I wish something would happen,' Rowena grumbled.

No sooner had the words left her mouth than there was a muffled cry, a pause, and then some fierce moving of the heather as someone wriggled the last part of the way up to them.

'Toby?' Lynette whispered.

His face was flushed, and he pushed his damp hair out of his eyes impatiently. 'They didn't see me, did they? I came to tell you. We've got proof now, but we can't use *Shona* to get back. The Rammers are over there. They've found *Shona*. Did you see them keeping watch on the hill?' He ran out of breath, and gasped. 'Roddy and Neil are getting *Seaspray*.'

'But . . .' Lynette began, and then pulled Rowena down as she started up in excitement.

On the high ground on the other side of the house three people appeared, moving swiftly down towards it.

'Roddy says to stay hidden here until he and Neil land on Falcon Island,' Toby whispered hoarsely. 'Then we go one at a time down to the nearest bit of shoreline and wait.'

It sounded simple, but they knew it wasn't. Toby

stared intently at the narrow strip of water between the two islands. Rowena, the rain running in rivulets down her flushed cheeks, gazed at the hillside on the other side of the house. She couldn't see anyone now, but any minute they might reappear.

Lynette thought of the currents in the water between the islands, and of the rocky shoreline beneath their own hill. How could they possibly bring *Seaspray* close enough in to take the three of them aboard?

The rain was harder now, blotting out the sea, and some of the other islands too.

'I can see them again,' Rowena said, her voice close to Lynette's ear. 'They've come out of the house . . . they're carrying boxes down to their boat. Oh come *on* Roddy and Neil!'

'Roddy's in the water, and Neil . . . half way across,' Toby squeaked. 'Look, they're swimming fast! Now they're there . . . they're on Falcon Island. Let's get going!'

It wasn't far, but it seemed a million miles as they wriggled down the hillside to the nearest rocky shore. Rowena, in the middle, bit her lip till it bled as she pulled herself along. Toby was last, trying hard not to chivvy her, and keeping a good look-out all round. He couldn't see any of the Rammers from here anyway, but he knew that three of them were going in the other direction towards the jetty, piling those important boxes into their boat to take them off for good. They all knew how important it was for them to get the news to Uncle Alec as soon as possible so they could be caught.

One or two large boulders near the rocky edge of the sea provided some shelter. The girls and Toby crouched down, making themselves as small as possible. Toby's deep excited breathing sounded loud in Lynette's ear. They couldn't see far now for the misty rain that greyed everything.

'Why don't we pray?' Rowena asked suddenly.

Lynette's heart thudded. She had been praying secretly ever since they landed here on Mellera More but to hear Rowena's words filled her with such a burst of joy she almost forgot why they needed God's help so desperately.

'Out loud?' Toby asked in dismay.

Lynette knew he approved really so she took the lead. 'Please God, help us,' she said. 'Please help us to get back safely . . . and to be in time to stop those people doing wrong to Coronsay. For your name's sake . . .'

'Amen,' the others joined in.

They kept silent for a moment. Lynette knew this was an important moment for Rowena, and she thanked God for helping her.

Toby saw the dark shadow of *Seaspray* first, and let out one seagull call *attention*! to guide Neil and Roddy to them.

'They're here!' Rowena whispered exultantly as she got up on one leg.

'Get ready to jump first, Lynette,' Toby said urgently. 'I'll help Rowena.'

They were in. Roddy had the paddle, and was using it furiously to keep them away from the rocks.

Neil, in the bows, held the mast and tried desperately to get it into place.

'Let *me*!' Rowena cried.

'Not with that ankle,' Neil said, still struggling.

The mast was up now. Rowena reached for the sail bag to pull out the sails. The three life-jackets were there, too. She thrust one each at Lynette, Toby and Neil.

'Not for me,' said Neil, busy with the jib. 'You wear it, Rowena, because of your ankle. Put it on.'

She didn't argue.

The centreboard was down now, making more room. Once the mast was up Neil had to stand to fix the boom in position and feed the mainsail in. Toby was ready to hold the jib sheet.

'I'll helm,' said Rowena, her voice strong. 'Sit opposite him, Neil. Roddy and Lynette in the middle of the boat, and get ready to come fast if we heel too much. We're going to have to tack. Hold tight!'

'Your ankle!' cried Neil. 'You'll never do it.'

'I *will*!'

'You can't!'

Rowena took no notice, and Neil could do no more. They had seemed to take so long, but now they moved fast.

Lynette's mouth was dry, and she bit her lip as a sudden gust hit them and nearly had them over. Roddy came up immediately beside Rowena who gripped the tiller hard.

Further out the conditions worsened. The heaving sea slapped over the blunt bows. The rain lashed their faces as they rushed towards the invisible mainland.

Lynette clung on to the centreboard case desperately, trying hard not to cry out in terror in the mad rush of bodies from side to side each time they went about. *Seaspray*, straining and shuddering through the waves, was doing her very best.

'Ready about?' Rowena shouted again, but now her voice was hoarse. The wind was coming off the mainland when they started, and it was all she had to navigate. But it could change, and what would happen then? One foot, her good one, was under the toe-strap to keep her in the boat as she leaned far out.

'An engine!' Toby yelled above the roaring wind. 'I heard an engine. They're after us.'

Fact, or imagination? No one knew. There was nothing they could do anyway except pray and keep going. Toby ducked as a sheet of sea water enveloped him, and then brushed a strand of dripping hair out of his eyes before another wave burst.

'Don't panic!' Rowena cried out.

They all suspected the Rammers were there, terrifyingly close. Roddy, for one, had no doubts of their intentions. Nothing would look more like an accident . . . *Seaspray* holed on the rocks, and themselves washed up on rocky shores in the next few days. Who would suspect it was deliberate? He gritted his teeth, and urged Rowena on though he knew she was doing her best in extremely dangerous conditions.

'Land ahead!' Neil cried, peering through the mist.

At once a loud crack had them all ducking. *Seaspray* rocked frantically and then lurched as the mast and sail came down.

'A shackle's broken,' Rowena cried in anguish, bringing the tiller round ineffectively. 'I can't do anything!'

The next minute they crashed against the rocks. Water poured in.

'Get out!' Rowena screamed. 'Get to the shore . . .'

It all happened so quickly. Lynette got a mouthful of water, and heard Rowena gasping behind her. The rocky shore was comfortably close. Half-stumbling, the girls pulled themselves out of the water and across the seaweed-slimy rocks that stung their wet bodies. Rowena, gasping in pain from her ankle, collapsed on the sand.

'Where's Neil?' cried Toby, coming up behind them.

Roddy wasn't there either. Toby scrambled back across the rocks to find them. Lynette started to go back, too. The rain had stopped now and visibility was better. She saw Roddy and Toby close by, half-dragging Neil along between them.

She rushed forward to help, slithering over the rocks. 'Is he hurt?'

As she reached them Toby stumbled and fell. He was up at once, but he was staggering. Lynette caught hold of him, and as they reached the firm sand near Rowena he threw himself down beside Neil.

Roddy's hat had gone, and his wet hair was plastered

to his head. 'I'm off to Butallie for help,' he cried. 'Lie low in case the mist clears.' He looked round wildly. There was no sight of the Rammer's boat, but the cloud was lifting and *Seaspray*, leaning drunkenly on the rocks, would soon be visible for miles.

He was off at once across the rough ground, but before the others had time to do as he said he was back. From his grim face they knew that something was badly wrong.

'It's too far to swim for it, and the current's too strong. I won't have a chance of getting there. They'll see me for sure and find you too. We can't get to Butallie. We can't stop them after all. We're on Coronsay!'

Chapter Sixteen

'Coronsay!' Lynette cried in horror. The shock of it took her breath away.

Toby gave a low groan, and sank back on the sand beside Neil. 'The wind changed,' he said. 'That's what went wrong. And then the shackle broke.'

Such a small thing, Lynette thought, to ruin everything.

'We won't give up,' Toby said with determination. 'We'll get to the top of Ben Vara and signal.'

'No one understands seagull signals, only us,' Neil said. He sat up gingerly, and checked that his camera was safe on its strap round his neck.

'You wouldn't listen to me yesterday,' Rowena stormed. 'We need another way of signalling, that's what I said. What good are seagull signals now? Nobody can hear us from here, and they wouldn't understand if they did.'

Roddy pushed his wet hair out of his eyes. 'They wouldn't see us either. It's too misty up there, right enough.'

'I'm going up there anyway,' said Toby, leaping up.

'Me too,' Lynette said. What good it would do she didn't know, but they had to do something.

They were off at once, keeping their heads down just in case.

Suddenly it came to Lynette what they must do. 'Toby,' she cried. 'It hasn't rained here. The heather's dry. We'll light a beacon fire.'

'Get the matches in Shanvara,' he shouted back. 'Hurry!'

Lynette gave a sob of relief as she reached for the matches on the shelf inside Shanvara and found them. Pausing only to grab up a handful of crisp dry bracken and as much driftwood as she could carry, she darted out of Shanvara to race up the hill.

Toby was there before her, tugging at the stalks of heather and shouting at her to be quick. Across the water Uncle Alec's cottage looked deserted in the clearing mist. So near, yet so far away.

'Oh let them be looking,' she gasped, as she threw down the kindling and struck a match. With a tiny splutter it went out. She tried again, sheltering it with her hand. A small flame caught at the dry bracken, flared for a moment and went out. Frantically she tried again. This time the bracken gave a little sizzle, and a gentle flame licked the dry wood.

The flames strengthened, reaching this way and that. All of a sudden the fire went up with a roar. Toby grabbed a handful of heather, and fed it on. It smoked for a moment, then glowed red and burnt fiercely.

'We've done it!' Toby shouted, leaping up and down. He grabbed more heather. 'They must see it from the cottage, they *must!*' He snatched off his orange lifejacket and waved it frantically above his head. Lynette joined him, and they danced up and down desperately.

At last there was the sign of movement over at the cottage as the door opened and two people came out, moving quickly down towards the harbour.

They were down on the beach before Uncle Alec's boat got to them. Toby shouted wildly for Uncle Alec to hurry as he waded into the water waving his arms. Lynette felt hot tears well up in her throat as she followed him. The engine cut out, and the anchor went down.

'Easy there,' came Uncle Alec's calm voice. 'Are you all here somewhere? Roddy and the Havills too?'

'Quick,' Lynette gasped.

'Get the police,' Toby cried. 'We've got proof of . . . those people, they're up to something and . . .'

'No need,' called another voice, and there was the elderly man, Mr Downing, in the boat too. 'Where are they?' he asked Lynette.

She stared back at him, unable for a moment to take in his being here. 'The Mellon Isles,' she gasped. 'On the biggest island, Mellera More. Oh, quickly, or they'll get away.'

As Uncle Alec helped the two of them aboard, Mr Downing held a mobile phone to his mouth and spoke into it. 'Roddy and the Havills?' Uncle Alec asked urgently. 'Where are they? Are they safe?'

She nodded. Just to see Uncle Alec's familiar figure and to feel his arm around her made her feel better. 'There, lass, there. You're safe now.'

'They're wet through too. The boat's damaged. We had to wade ashore on the other side of Coronsay. That's where they are.'

At once he was over the side, wading quickly ashore. Lynette felt suddenly sick with relief as Neil came bounding across the sand. '*Wow*!' he shouted, staring up at Ben Vara in awe.

Uncle Alec set off quickly, returning with Roddy and Rowena, the two of them helping her as she hobbled between them. Her face was flushed and her eyes bright. They all gazed up at the blazing hill.

'We've set it on fire,' Toby yelled from the boat. 'Coronsay's on fire!'

The others stood in a wet bedraggled group, their faces glowing in the warmth.

'Time to go,' Uncle Alec said. He looked anxiously at Rowena's swollen ankle, and then picked her up without a word and carried her to the boat. This time she didn't object. Neil followed, and was helped aboard too. Uncle Alec pushed off from the shore and then climbed in.

They huddled together, their teeth chattering. Behind them the island of Coronsay was a blazing mass. Tears ran down Lynette's face, but she didn't care. What did it matter? They were safe, but Coronsay, their beautiful Coronsay, was burning and she and Toby had done it.

She sobbed quietly against Mr Downing's tweed-jacketed shoulder.

Chapter Seventeen

'We've got them,' said Mr Downing. 'They're safe in custody.'

There was an excited clamour as they all tried to speak at once and eat their soup at the same time. They were in the small kitchen at the cottage, all crowded together because Mr and Mrs Havill were there too. Aunt Ruth, at the stove, was stirring the soup left in the pan, ready for second helpings. They had never tasted anything so good.

They looked an odd crew, all of them dressed in an assortment of clothes. As soon as they arrived at the cottage, dripping wet and shivering, Aunt Ruth had taken one horrified look at them and bundled them inside without waiting for explanations.

'First things first,' she said. 'There's plenty of hot water. We'll hear all about it when you're clean and dry. Thank God you're safe. Alec's been on the lookout for you since the cloud came down. He left the boat ready at the jetty to go out again.'

They didn't take long because they were all bursting to talk. The doctor had been summoned by Mr Downing, and Rowena's ankle was now bandaged again and arrangements made for a visit to hospital in Inverness next day.

Neil's fair hair was standing up in peaks because he had towelled it dry but forgotten to comb it. Roddy, in a pair of Uncle Alec's trousers and a jacket two sizes too large, was white and drawn. Lynette looked at him anxiously. She hadn't meant to set the whole of Coronsay on fire. She knew what he must be feeling as he glanced at the red glow through the window. The flames had died down a little now but the island was well and truly alight.

'Yes, we've got them,' Mr Downing said in satisfaction.

'But how?' Neil asked. 'I mean . . . who *are* you? Roddy's Mum said you didn't work any more. So you *are* in the police?'

Mr Downing smiled at him. 'They called me in for this special case. I know this area well, you see, so I was the man for the job.'

Neil grinned. 'We wondered about you. We thought you might be one of them.'

Mr Downing smiled. 'Did I look as if I might have been stealing plants from your island?'

'You could have been in disguise.'

'True. And so I was, in a way, by being myself. It was natural for me to accept Colonel Murdoch's invitation to stay with him as I'd often done in the past. No one would suspect what I was really up to. And with your help we were able to pull it off. Now *you've* got some explaining to do.'

'We had to do it,' Lynette said quickly. 'We had to light the fire. They'd have got away . . .'

'An excellent plan, but I didn't mean that. How did you discover what those people were doing?'

And then they were all explaining about following the Rammers to the Mellon Isles, and Roddy recognising two of them who had rented Mrs Crawford's cottage last week. They told him about finding the rows of cultivated coronwort plants, and the powder in boxes they had discovered inside the house.

'We brought some back with us,' said Neil. 'I wanted to photograph the boxes but . . .' His eyes clouded as he thought of his camera. Had water got in and ruined the film?

'Don't worry about your camera,' said Uncle Alec. 'I had a look at it while you were upstairs. We've got the film out and it should be all right.'

'We left *Shona* and came in *Seaspray* . . .' said Toby. He broke off, thinking of the sailing dinghy on the rocks.

'We've discovered the dinghy, and Roddy's boat too,' said Mr Downing.

'And you've caught the Rammers,' Neil cried, handing up his bowl for a third helping.

'We've been watching for them for days,' said Mr Downing. 'We knew something was going on in this vast remote area. Any lead was welcome, however small, the silver penknife . . .'

'Have you still got it?' Toby asked.

Mr Downing smiled, and produced it from his pocket. 'Who knows if this set the whole thing off . . . maybe they returned to look for it the time you saw them? A small thing, but significant. Your finding the flower you were unable to identify set me thinking. I did try to warn you to keep well clear.'

'But what were they doing with it?' Rowena demanded as she put her spoon down in her empty bowl and took a scone.

Mr Downing hesitated, looking at her thoughtfully. 'I'm coming to that. Can I trust you to keep what I'm going to tell you to yourselves?'

They all nodded, and Toby's eyes widened with excitement.

'Those Rammers of yours knew how to make a dangerous drug from coronwort. That's why they were collecting and planting it. It grows nowhere else in the world. I can't begin to tell you how vitally important it was for us to catch them. Their contact ship was waiting for them out at sea, but they never reached it. We had officers stationed all along the coast. They didn't stand a chance once we knew from you where they were operating from.'

'But I don't understand how you children did it,' Mrs Havill said, looking from one to the other in bewilderment. 'How did Rowena manage to helm with her foot like that?'

It was no problem explaining it all again.

'Rowena did a great job,' said Neil enthusiastically. 'No one else could have done it.'

Rowena flushed with pleasure as they all agreed.

'It was a good thing Neil insisted we didn't leave her behind on Mellera More,' Roddy said.

Mrs Havill paled. 'Leave her behind?'

'Only because it was safer for her to stay hidden.'

'Those people are dangerous . . .' her father broke off in horror.

'But Neil wouldn't leave without her.'

'I should hope not.' Rowena's mother seemed close to tears. She bit her lip, and looked down at her lap.

Rowena stared at her, appalled. 'Oh, *Mum*!' The next moment she was in Mrs Havill's arms with her head pressed against her shoulder. 'It's all right, Mum, really it is,' she said after a moment as her mother released her, but she looked at her brother strangely. 'You said that, Neil, about not leaving me behind? But why?'

Neil looked awkward. 'You're my sister, aren't you? Anyway I knew Mum and Dad would be mad at me.'

Lynette looked at the four of them, and it seemed to her as if the family were all alone in the room.

Then Mrs Havill spoke huskily. 'I'm proud of my daughter getting you all back safely. Well done, Rowena!'

'But I didn't,' she said. '*Seaspray*'s holed very badly.'

Mr Downing stood up and went to the window to gaze at Coronsay's red glow. Then he turned his back on it, and looked at them gravely.

'As I said coronwort is an important little plant. Just how important nobody knew until you showed us. The sailing dinghy will be brought to the harbour in the morning. Let me know the damage and we'll see what can be done. And maybe we'll provide another camera, too.' His eyes twinkled. 'An under-water camera might be a good idea.' He smiled warmly at Toby who was still spooning soup into his mouth as if he hadn't eaten for months. 'And I have a feeling that another sailing dinghy will be provided for you and your sister, lad.'

Toby gulped and spluttered. 'For us? You really mean it?'

Lynette smiled too, pleased for Toby. It was what he had always wished for. She looked quickly at Rowena. Rowena always wanted things to be fair, so what was she thinking?

She needn't have worried. Rowena's dark eyes were shining, and her face glowed. Happiness radiated from her as she smiled at her father.

Neil, looking as if his face had been newly scrubbed, was making plans for races round Coronsay. But Roddy was staring broodingly across the water at the burning island.

'Aye, Coronsay's safe now, lad,' Uncle Alec said, following his gaze. 'No more people stealing plants.'

'No more plants to steal,' Lynette said. 'I only meant to light a beacon fire . . .'

'Not to worry.' Roddy turned to smile at her. 'Coronsay's been cleansed by fire. The young shoots of heather will grow again next year, right enough, and coronwort too.'

'But we might not be here next year.' She thought suddenly of the worry about their new home that had been pushed to the back of her mind. But now, somehow, it felt different. A challenge as Dad said, just as helping Rowena had been a challenge that had come brilliantly right. Their new life could be brilliant, too, with God's help. She smiled back at Rowena.

Mr Downing was buttoning up his tweed jacket and looking round for his walking stick. 'There's something in the pipeline,' he said, 'but keep it under your hats, even if you've lost yours, Roddy. Remind me to buy you another one, by the way. It's likely that island of yours will be kept as some kind of nature reserve in the future. Your uncle here, and Roddy, might be wardens . . . yourselves, too, when you can be here. How does that strike you?'

Neil gave a shout of delight, and thumped Toby in the back so his spoon fell with a clatter. 'It'll be like our own island!'

Roddy had a special look in his eyes. 'No one else will try to rob Coronsay, ever.'

Mr and Mrs Havill were getting up now and chivvying their family. 'We'll take Roddy with us,' said Mr Havill. 'Mr Downing too. Plenty of time to talk this over tomorrow. Come on, Rowena, let me help you. You were a courageous girl in those terrible conditions.'

Rowena grinned, her hair sticking damply to her head. 'And I didn't get into trouble frightening everybody like the first time.'

Left alone with their uncle and aunt, Lynette and Toby looked at each other, hardly able to believe all that had happened.

'Coronsay a nature reserve,' Lynette said dreamily. 'I'm glad it's all over. I liked finding out about coronwort best. Now I'll study all the wildlife on Coronsay . . .' she broke off and yawned.

They went to the window in time to see the Havills' car disappear round the bend in the narrow road.

'We'll need to make lots of plans,' Toby cried.

Lynette didn't answer. In her mind she was far away, over there on Coronsay. The island seemed to her to be no longer charred and blackened but sprouting green with new life.